The Dark Fae

(The World of Fae)

Book 1

TERRY SPEAR

Discover more about Terry Spear at:
http://www.terryspear.com

DEDICATION

To my daughter, Jennifer, and her love of fantasy.

ACKNOWLEDGMENTS

Thanks to my Rebel Romance Writers for always being there for me!

CHAPTER 1

Alicia hadn't left her girlfriend sunbathing on the South Padre Island beach for more than a few minutes when another hot guy approached Cassie—only this one worried her.

He had dark fae written all over him. Well, maybe not written all over him, but the medallion he wore clued her in immediately.

After grabbing the ice-cold sodas from the snack stand, Alicia trudged back through the mounds of hot sand at record speed, trying not to spill their drinks on the white sugar beach. Cassie still lay on her back on her playful seal beach towel next to Alicia's colorful golden dragon.

Already five guys had hit on Cassie.

What was it with her and guys? It was if Cassie wore a neon sign that stated in bold, colorful, flashing letters, "Come play with me."

Was it the way she smiled in such a heartwarming fashion? Not to mention the fit of her hot pink bikini on that silky tanned body of hers. Or the way her dark brown curls whipped around her bare shoulders by the Gulf breeze and her equally dark brown eyes smiled at the guys.

Alicia glanced down at the oversized tie-dyed shirt that covered her pale body. Her shimmering blue bikini and curves could catch the guys' eyes, too, except if she exposed her skin for a few minutes in the sun's hot rays, she'd be redder than her mother's roses. Best to hide the bikini rather than ruin her summer vacation with a roasting hot sunburn.

When Alicia grew closer to their claimed speck of sandy territory, the dark-haired guy drew her attention again. He, of course, had eyes only for Cassie.

This one was different from the other guys though.

This one exuded danger and at once Alicia's internal alarm bells sounded. He was built rock solid, though he appeared to be around seventeen or so like she and Cassie. But the medallion lying flat against his naked chest, the gold disk catching the sun's rays...the symbol of the royal house of Denkar of fae kind—forced a chill down her spine, despite the sun beating on her bare arms.

His dark hair and eyes and dangerous smile signified he was of the dark fae, the hunter class, the ones who caused more mischief among the human mortals than any other.

Only this time, he'd targeted the wrong human.

Alicia had always considered it a curse that she could see one of the fae in their invisible form because they appeared semi-translucent at the edges. And likewise she could recognize them when they were solidly visible as the golden ring around their eyes glowed like a burning flame when they were angered, or sparkled like shimmering faery dust when they were not. In this case, the medallion etched with a lion's head—the same one she'd seen described in her father's journal—indicated the dark fae belonged to the Denkar.

For the moment, she hoped her abilities might be able to save her friend from pain and suffering. But the situation could turn into catastrophic consequences for her if he discovered she knew he was of the fae kind.

The six-foot tall faery towered over Cassie as she sat up on her towel. His dark wet hair curled at his broad shoulders and his golden tanned chest glistened with water droplets from the Gulf. He was beautiful. Dimples appeared when he smiled and laughed, the sound deeply sensual, drawing Cassie under his spell. And Alicia, too, if she didn't snap out of it. What she wouldn't give to have a boyfriend who looked like...

She shook her head at herself. The fae killed her kind—those who had the ability to see the fae who were not immortal like them. Her father had said so.

Cassie was getting ready to stand when Alicia reached the two of them, intent on thwarting the faery.

When targeting its intended victim, the fae appeared incredibly one-track minded. Because of this, the Denkar fae didn't see Alicia arrive only feet away from him. For the moment, he had eyes only for Cassie.

For the moment.

He certainly couldn't have expected two cups of icy, sweet sodas to fly in his direction. But when the cold, dark drinks splashed against his naked, golden chest—that got his attention.

Or rather Alicia's attention.

"Oh, sorry." She tried to keep the giggles under wrap, unsuccessfully.

Cassie glowered at her.

The fae's glare worried Alicia more as the golden rings around his dark brown eyes glowed brightly. She'd definitely pissed off one royal faery hunter, and she expected payback to be hell.

"Uhm, Cassie, don't you think we ought to be going?" Alicia glanced at her wrist, intending to tell Cassie it was time for lunch, but remembered too late she'd left her watch back at the hotel.

Cassie opened her mouth to speak, then turned to look at the dark caramelized carbonated drinks dribbling down the fae's chest toward a pair of shimmering blue swim trunks. Then she looked back at Alicia. Cassie probably couldn't believe Alicia would ignore what she'd just done to the fae. "Deveron has asked me to go to lunch with him. He's here for a week of summer vacation also."

"No, you can't! I mean..." Alicia was blowing her cover big time.

Deveron's square jaw tightened as his eyes darkened.

Not good.

"I mean, okay. So where are we going?" Alicia figured neither Cassie nor the fae intended to take her along for the ride. Especially after she anointed him with the sugary drinks. But somehow she had to protect her friend.

Cassie glanced at Deveron, then back at Alicia. "Well, he only asked me. I hope it's okay with you, Alicia."

His glare remained fixed on Alicia the whole time.

Will of nerves?

She couldn't let the hunter know she knew exactly what he was. For too many millennia his kind had destroyed her kind. She had no intention of being the next statistic.

Should she let the fae play with Cassie's heart, then break it? Certainly it would be less painful than what Alicia would have to go through if the dark fae knew what she was capable of doing and decided to terminate her.

Nope.

Friends took care of friends and Alicia wasn't about to let some hunk of a fae hurt Cassie.

Even though at the moment, Cassie appeared pretty annoyed with her and didn't seem to want Alicia's help in the matter.

Alicia had never met another human who could see the fae like she could either. Though she'd always wondered about her father. He'd abandoned her mother when Alicia was five. But the journal he'd left behind, describing an unreal faery world, made her think he had the ability like her. That's how she knew the dark faeries hunted the humans who could see them. And that's how she knew about the various royal houses scattered across the States each with their own symbol-embossed medallions.

But her mother never spoke of her father after he'd called it quits with her early one spring morning. That was the last Alicia had seen him.

The faery finally glanced at Cassie and smiled warmly, but the smile never reached his eyes. "I'll take a dip in the water to rinse off, then join you at your room in a few minutes." He turned to look at Alicia as he continued to speak to Cassie. "Bring your friend. It could be extremely—*interesting*."

His deep voice was meant to be perfectly sensual, disarming, luring, but Alicia sensed the deadliness to his tone.

The fae usually only targeted one human at a time. But she was certain he'd make an exception in her case.

Not only would he attempt to break Cassie's heart, he'd destroy Alicia's friendship with her. She would bet her small savings on it. Oh, then he'd destroy her.

Not good.

Cassie smiled at Deveron until he turned and stalked toward the aqua, crystal clear water. Then she grabbed her beach towel and shook the sand from it with more vigor than was necessary. "What was that all about? I've never seen you act so clumsy. And then you didn't even have the decency to apologize to Deveron. Not only that, but he asked me to go to lunch, not you. Why couldn't you have politely made excuses? Even if he had been nice enough to invite you, too, why would he after the way you acted toward him?"

Alicia studied the fae as he waded into the water. How could she thwart him?

But when he turned and caught her eye, she quickly grabbed her beach towel, avoiding any further eye contact. "He's a heartbreaker, Cassie. I saw him kissing a blond yesterday," she lied, hating to, but not knowing how else to warn Cassie the guy wasn't an ordinary guy and he was evil to the core. "And the day before that, he had his arms wrapped securely around a redhead—a much *older* redhead."

"Oh?" Cassie's voice was laced with skepticism. "I never saw him."

Neither had Alicia.

Then a golden-haired male fae walked toward her, wearing a green silky tunic, criss-crossed with leather ties, and butternut breeches. This one wasn't visible to humans. Well, most humans. She quickly averted her eyes so he wouldn't know she'd seen him.

Her attention shifted to Deveron. His dark brows knit together in a deep frown as he watched her. Did he realize she saw the golden-haired fae? She could have been looking at nothing, the Gulf, the people sunbathing down the beach, a seagull.

She cursed herself inwardly. Better that Cassie have a broken heart, then Alicia face the wrath of a hunter fae who'd seek to destroy her for her abilities.

She took a deep breath of the humid air, saturated with the smell of saltwater and fish. "Listen, Cassie, you're right. You go out with Deveron on your own. Just be careful. And you know me. I'll manage just fine."

As much as she hated to let the fae win at his game with Cassie, it was probably best for all concerned.

"If you'd remove that bulky T-shirt, you'd have guys asking you out also." Cassie smiled.

"Remember last year? I tried sunbathing on a beach towel like you do. *And* I got so badly burned I couldn't move in sunlight for three days as if I was a vampire who would turn into a pile of ashes. Heck, Cassie, it's just not worth it."

Cassie nodded. "Yeah, I remember. Then you peeled like a shedding snake for days afterward."

"Yep, I was just as cute as could be."

Cassie laughed. "All right, well, thanks, Alicia. I really appreciate your bowing out like this."

"Yeah, just remember what I said about him. He's not to be trusted. Three different girls on three different days doesn't say much for his stick-to-it-ness."

"It's just for lunch." Cassie tucked her beach towel under her arm and grinned at Alicia. "You're the best friend ever."

Not really. If Alicia were Cassie's best friend, she'd glue herself to Cassie's side. Not run away in the face of danger.

She glanced over her shoulder at the dark fae, who studied her every action. Her heart beat harder and her hands grew clammy.

He was tall, dark, genuinely handsome, and the worst kind of danger.

10

CHAPTER 2

Deveron, crown prince of the fae kingdom of Denkar, rubbed his naturally smooth cheek as he considered the petite blonde's backside. She wore a dowdy T-shirt and hid how she truly looked, and he normally wouldn't have given her a second glance. He was much more intrigued with a girl like Cassie. But what really grabbed his attention was the strict animosity Cassie's girlfriend had shown toward him—as if she knew just what he was and what he had planned for her friend. A case of jealousy? Or something that went deeper?

He'd sent his bodyguard Herlenkis in close to her to see her reaction and he couldn't decide. It was as if she had seen him, and then quickly realized her mistake and had tried to cover up her reaction.

He had to know for certain. The way she looked at Deveron's medallion and acted so hostile toward him, he swore she knew what he was up to, what he was, and where he was from.

Yet how could she?

Mortal humans had no way of knowing about the immortal fae. But the way her gaze shifted to observe his bodyguard, forced him to consider otherwise. What if by some strange coincidence, she could indeed see his people?

He glanced up the beach. A hundred yards away, Herlenkis

studied bathing beauties, tanning under the strong rays of the sun.

"Herlenkis!"

The golden-haired fae turned to face him.

Deveron motioned for him to join him in the water.

Herlenkis vanished, then reappeared chest deep next to him in the gentle swells of the Gulf. "Yes, my lord?"

"I have a task for you. Get Tandora. We have a date."

"Date, my lord? You know what Queen Irenis said about stirring up the humans."

Deveron cocked a brow as he folded his arms. "Do you not work for me?" He was the crown prince after all, and he had hand-picked Herlenkis for his loyalty and his good natured ways—for a dark fae.

"Yes, my lord."

"Good, remember that." Deveron considered asking Herlenkis if he had ever known of a human who could see the fae, but dismissed the notion. He had no intention of telling anyone his plans, yet. If the girl could see them, she'd expose her abilities within the hour. Then he could have some real fun. But not with Cassie as he'd intended. With Alicia instead.

Herlenkis looked after the two girls, turned to Deveron, bowed low, then vanished.

In fact, it didn't really concern Deveron if Alicia knew what he was. Because she had anointed him with sticky sodas, she was all his to do with as he pleased. Didn't matter if the queen had forbidden him to trifle with the human girls.

This one had declared war on him. To think she hadn't even apologized, just stood there trying to suppress a giggle as her blue eyes sparkled with pixie mirth.

He looked back at the stucco Spanish-style hotel as the sunlight glinted off the red tile roof. When his reinforcements arrived, he'd see if she thought the situation was truly that funny any longer.

He smiled, dove under the water, then vanished.

* * *

Alicia tugged off her oversized T-shirt as Cassie took her shower first. The salt and sand felt grimy on her skin and hair, and she couldn't wait to wash it all off.

Cassie sang some nonsensical tune at the top of her lungs. Alicia shook her head and smiled.

But then her smile turned bitter.

More than anything, she wanted to stop the fae from hurting her friend. But how could she? She had no idea where Deveron was taking Cassie for lunch even.

Maybe she could find out before they left. Then she could follow them. *Maybe.*

Cassie walked out of the bathroom with a white towel wrapped around her head, the rest of her dressed in a pale green dress, her feet still bare. "Your turn."

Alicia glanced at the door to their room. "If he comes before I'm finished showering, let me know where you're going to lunch."

"Worry wart."

Alicia frowned at her.

"All right. Get cleaned up. I promise I'll tell you before I go."

Would the fae distract Cassie enough so she didn't remember to tell Alicia? That's what worried her. She hurried into the shower, intending to take the quickest one she could.

The whole time the peach-scented soap slipped over her skin, she listened for the sound of Cassie speaking, or the fae's dark voice penetrating the quiet.

Nothing.

She turned off the shower, then quickly dried her skin. Then she realized all she'd brought into the bathroom was a change of panties and bra and the long T-shirt she wore to bed.

She threw them on, then hurried out of the room.

Cassie raised a brow. "You're going to bed?"

"No." Alicia couldn't help the annoyance in her voice. "I forgot to take a change of clothes in there." She yanked on a pair of jeans shorts, then as she pulled the nightshirt off, a knocking on the door sent her heart skittering.

Before Alicia could pull her nightshirt back on or dart for the bathroom, Cassie yanked the door open.

But Deveron's eyes didn't focus on Cassie. Instead he concentrated on Alicia, who covered her lacy bra and dashed into the bathroom, cursing under her breath.

She swore she heard the fae chuckle. But what was worse, two blond-haired males accompanied him. What had he intended to do to poor Cassie?

Luckily, though she saw the others as clearly as she saw Deveron, she had the foresight not to look directly at them. Still, the notion he'd brought reinforcements disconcerted her.

"Alicia wants to know where we're going for lunch, you know, in case my parents call while I'm out," Cassie said to Deveron as Alicia paced across the bathroom tile floor.

She had no shirt to cover her at all now and was stuck in here until the fae and his friends left.

"She's not going with us?" Deveron asked, his tone of voice surprised.

Why would he be surprised? She knew he hated her for what she'd done to him. And surely he didn't want her to tag along. Or did he?

Sure, for revenge after what she'd pulled. After all, he was a royal fae, and she was certain not too many would have risked insulting him by dousing him with very ice cold sodas.

"Well, I thought that you wouldn't care for her to join us," Cassie said. She sounded irritated.

"No, have her come along, too. I have a friend who will meet us at the Mexican restaurant."

A friend. Hmpf. Another fae.

But then again, if she went with them, she could try and keep Cassie safe.

Only she had to get rid of Deveron for now so she could put a shirt on.

Cassie knocked on the bathroom door. "Did you hear that Alicia?

Do you want to go?"

"Sure, but have Deveron..." She almost slipped and said something about his companions. "Have Deveron step outside of the room so I can get dressed."

"Oh, oh, sure."

With a voice as smooth as heavy satin, Deveron said, "I'll be waiting in the lobby."

"Okay, fine," Cassie said, sugary sweet.

When the door clicked close, Alicia yanked the bathroom door open, intending to get a change of clothes—and nearly died.

Standing in the center of the room watching her, was the first golden-haired fae she'd seen on the beach. His blue eyes narrowed as she faked looking right through him. *And* pretended to herself she was totally dressed and not exposing her bra-clad breasts to an immortal faery.

Jeez, her whole body heated with embarrassment.

They had no earthly feelings, she reminded herself. *He sees you as nothing more than a dumb dog.*

She dug through her garments hanging in the shared closet as goose bumps covered her arms, and her heart beat rapidly. Did the dark fae realize she knew they existed and this one was left behind to test her?

She was certain that was the reason.

This afternoon, she would have to put on the performance of a lifetime. Unfortunately, acting wasn't something she was good at.

As nonchalantly as she could, she pulled out a simple blue dress, smiled at Cassie, then stalked into the bathroom and shut the door.

"I was surprised he wanted you to go with us," Cassie said as she leaned against the door.

"Yeah, well, you heard him. He has a friend who needs to be entertained." The thought soured her. Sure he figured she'd be totally entertaining. Watch her squirm as she tried to pretend she couldn't see the other fae.

When she walked back into the room, the fae was sifting through her undergarments in one of the drawers in a chest.

She could have screamed. And she knew that's just why he was rummaging through them—to get a reaction from her.

He looked up in the mirror at her. Again, his eyes narrowed.

She quickly leaned down to slip on a pair of heeled sandals.

Grabbing Cassie's arm, she said, "Ready to go?" She worried her face appeared as red as chili peppers because her cheeks were so hot.

"Hungry?" Cassie asked as they stepped into the hall. Then she closed the door to their room.

Alicia had been, but for now, she was way too keyed up to be hungry at all. "Sure."

Footsteps sounded behind them, but she refused to look back. If whoever it was proved to be the fae, he'd realize for certain she knew he existed because she could hear the movement of an invisible fae, when she shouldn't be able to.

When they arrived at the lobby, palm tree and ferns nearly hid the fae from her sight. In fact, when she saw the dark fae, she imagined he felt right at home among the lush greenery.

Deveron's gaze took in her blond hair, blue dress, and strappy sandals as he crossed the white marble floor to greet her. He barely looked at Cassie. Was he already trying to form a rift between Alicia and her friend?

He glanced at the fae she imagined stood behind her as she could feel his warm breath touching her bare shoulder.

Deveron smiled.

Had the blond-haired fae told Deveron using some kind of facial expression that she was indeed startled to see him in her hotel room? Could they telepathically communicate?

Maybe going out with Deveron and his cohorts wasn't such a great idea after all.

He motioned to the lobby doors. "Your carriage awaits, ladies."

He stepped in between Cassie and her, only his hand rested on Alicia's lower back as he guided them outside. She resented it, but when she tried to step away from him, one of the golden-haired faeries drew close so she couldn't move in any direction without running into him.

An invisible fae could slip right through her, giving her a strange tingling feeling like when her foot would fall asleep. She avoided bumping into faeries for that reason.

But when the fae began to speak, she blinked hard. She'd never heard an invisible fae speak before. Was he doing it for her benefit? To see her reaction?

"I believe your concern is warranted," the fae said, not speaking to Alicia, but to Deveron, though his blue eyes studied Alicia as he walked backward in front of her.

She tried to control where she looked, but avoiding looking at the creature could prove that she saw him, too.

"She's wily, my lord."

Deveron nodded. She figured he couldn't speak to the fae or confuse Cassie. So in a way, the dark fae was forced to playact also.

Good.

She was certain he was dying to ask the blond-haired fae more, but couldn't.

The other stood slightly shorter and had green eyes. He didn't pay much attention to either of the women, just led the party toward a black Ford Taurus.

She wondered when the royal fae had learned to drive a car.

Neither of the other two wore gold medallions. She assumed they served their lord, as the one had called him. That they were not members of the royal family. Or maybe they didn't always wear them in the human world.

Deveron opened the car door for Cassie, while Alicia yanked the back door open for herself. Before she could slide into the leather seat, the fae with the blue eyes slid in first and sat where she planned to.

She hesitated.

Deveron raised his brows at her when he shut Cassie's door.

Alicia groaned inwardly. No way did she want to sit on the fae. Her whole body would tingle all the way to the restaurant.

"Something wrong?" Deveron asked, his tone amused.

"No, nothing." She climbed on top of the fae and hoped she squished him good. As soon as she sat on him, she felt as though millions of nettles touched her skin, not painfully, but with an odd sort of prickling.

Deveron mouth curved in a small smile, then he shut her door. She was afraid he knew that she could see the fae.

When they arrived at the Mexican restaurant, Alicia played her cool role for all it was worth. After Deveron opened Cassie's car door, Alicia allowed him to open hers. And she purposely didn't jump out of the car, but took her time, though she was dying to get off the blond fae's lap.

Again, the dark fae's eyes and lips smiled at her in that devilish manner that seemed to be his trademark. His gaze shifted to the blond fae she knew stood behind her. What secret communication passed between them this time?

Had the blond fae enjoyed her sitting on his lap? Again, she felt her cheeks flush.

Deveron's hand drifted to the small of her back as he escorted them inside the restaurant. Smooth...really smooth. She attempted to slide away from his touch, but the blond fae from the beach appeared in front of her, giving her barely room to walk without stepping on his boot-clad heels.

A hostess seated them immediately due to the early lunch hour. Lively Spanish tunes played overhead as the smell of grilled beef scented the air conditioned room. Alicia's stomach rumbled.

Colorful sombreros, and cowboy boots decorated some of the walls, while others pictured murals of cactus and Spanish cowboys riding the range. But when she shifted her attention back to Deveron, she found he studied her still.

Cassie was already looking at her menu. Did she not notice the interest Deveron was paying Alicia? She could have kicked him for trying to upset her friendship with Cassie.

At the bare table, another blond fae, this one brown-eyed, joined them. He first looked at Deveron who nodded, then motioned to Cassie.

"This is Cassie."

Then he took Alicia's hand. "And this is Alicia. Meet Micala, my cousin."

Was Micala truly Deveron's cousin? The family resemblance was there, Alicia had to admit.

The new faery took in her appearance, just like Deveron had, but then he did the unexpected. He moved his seat closer to Cassie and began to talk to her low, so Alicia couldn't hear their words.

Cassie glanced at Deveron, who smiled broadly back at her. She must have felt he didn't mind if she talked to Micala. So Cassie turned her attention to him while Deveron faced Alicia. She imagined Deveron targeted her because she endangered him.

Now she was sure the inquisition would begin.

"Where are you from?" Deveron asked her.

The other fae watched her while Micala continued to distract Cassie.

Were they trying to figure out how she came to know they existed? She felt like a goldfish in a glass bowl with a lethal audience. The golden lion guard and the dark fae panther watched her, waiting for the right moment to pounce on her and eat her up.

"Sacramento, California."

"Who are your parents?"

She folded her arms. She wasn't about to put up with the third degree. "Who are yours?"

Deveron's dark brown eyes sparkled with amusement as he grinned. But the gold that ringed his eyes shimmered like iridescent faery dust, so she wasn't in too much danger...at the moment. Yet, she assumed he wouldn't want to reveal who his royal parents were and seemed amused she'd counter his question with one, too.

He sipped his water slowly, never taking his eyes off her. He was challenging her to a duel.

Slip up once and he'd have her terminated.

"How much do you know about us?" he asked.

"I don't know what you mean."

He set his glass down on the table. "Ahh, but you do."

He motioned to the blue-eyed faery, then held up the water glass to him. The faery moved close to Deveron and leaned over to hear his words spoken privately.

In response, the faery grinned, lifted the water glass, then walked over to Alicia. He began to tilt it toward her lap.

Immediately, she grabbed it from him and sat it back on the table.

"You weren't bothered by a floating glass of water?" Deveron leaned back in his seat. His eyes twinkled in the soft light. "Most would have been upset, but you saw Herlenkis carrying it toward you. Instead of observing him, you watched me. Why wouldn't you have watched the glass of water?"

"A magician's trick."

He smiled. Then he leaned forward against the edge of the table and pinched his dark brows together. "You will tell me everything I want to know. First and foremost, who your parents are. Or..." He glanced at Cassie, who was talking to Micala about the glorious beaches in Padre Island. "Your friend will. Your choice."

Again, a roguish grin creased his face as a glint of malice reflected in his dark eyes and the gold circle around them glowed brightly.

CHAPTER 3

Alicia sat taller and crossed her arms. No dark fae, royal or otherwise, would intimidate her with vague threats. But before she had time to tell him off, a female fae appeared next to him. The transparent edges of her body indicated she was invisible to humans like the two blond male faeries who hovered around the table.

Ice blue silky sheers covered an opaque shimmering gown that reached the female faery's ankles. Her hair coiled on top of her head like rich satiny brown rope and golden clasps decorated in sapphires held it in place. Her brown eyes were the same dark color and almond shape as Deveron's. But she had a small, pixie-sized face, rather than the handsome square jaw like Deveron had. She, like Deveron, wore an embossed gold medallion featuring a lion's head at her breast.

The whole time she only considered Deveron, ignoring his female human companions and the blond faeries as Deveron scowled back at her.

She quickly leaned over and whispered in Deveron's ear.

His eyes widened.

She nodded.

He took a ragged breath, then rose from his seat. "Ladies, business calls. I will drop by later to see you."

The female fae said, "You will *not*, Deveron."

Alicia's brows rose in amusement as he glanced at her. So the tough, ever-in-control Deveron could be ordered about by a female royal fae?

He pulled two twenties from his wallet and dropped them on the table. "Enjoy lunch."

"You don't think you can return after you take care of your business?" Cassie asked. She looked terribly disappointed.

Alicia sighed, deeply relieved the dark fae was leaving.

Micala kissed Cassie's cheek, and she smiled. "Later," he said, echoing Deveron's sentiments.

Deveron grasped Alicia's hand and squeezed. "I will know all about you, my faery princess." His dark eyes gleamed with mischief, warning her he wouldn't be trifled with.

"In your dreams," she said, her voice icy.

"I never sleep." His lips curved up at the corners slightly, then he hurried out of the dining area with Micala and the other two fae males.

The female remained behind and studied Alicia. She ignored Cassie, but Alicia assumed this was because the faery was of the royal house and only Deveron's interest in a particular human female would raise the dark fae's ire.

Was the fae his girlfriend then?

"Insipid human," the fae snarled.

"Jealous faery," Alicia responded back. Then her whole body warmed as the faery stared at her with her mouth partly dropped open. The golden rings around her dark brown eyes weren't glowing yet though. She must have been in shock to hear Alicia speak to her, and certainly Alicia was shocked that she'd let the words slip off her tongue.

Whatever had made her speak to the faery? And particularly those words. Envy? Nah. Why should she care if Deveron had the hots for his own kind? Certainly not when he thought he'd tell Alicia what she would and wouldn't do. And then he'd terminate her.

Alicia did what she should have done in the first place, ignored the haughty faery. "That was awfully nice of Deveron to pay for our lunches, Cassie. But I was thinking maybe we ought to save some of our money and return home early."

"Do not ignore me," the faery said to Alicia, fisting her hands on her hips.

"You've got to be kidding. We worked all year at the Pizzaria just to earn enough to take this vacation," Cassie said, then sipped her water.

Alicia nodded, knowing there was no way she'd ever convince Cassie to leave the resort early. She certainly couldn't tell her about the fae.

The faery growled when Alicia continued to pretend she didn't exist. When the waitress set chips and salsa on the table, took Alicia and Cassie's orders for beef fajitas, then left, Alicia said, "Do you want to go to a movie following lunch?"

The fae smiled an almost malevolent grin, then vanished.

Now what?

Cassie dipped a chip in hot sauce. "Yes, I'd like that."

A movie would keep them away from the hotel for a while if Deveron and Micala returned to their room to see them. But what was the female fae up to? She'd cause problems for sure.

Was she going to report back to their queen now that Deveron had entertained a human female who could see the fae kind? Would she issue the order to terminate Alicia sooner?

Maybe she should have spoken with the faery.

She glanced at Cassie. *No.* Cassie would have wondered who Alicia had been talking to.

When the steaming hot platters of sizzling beef strips, onions and green and red bell peppers arrived, so did the royal female fae.

Only this time she was visible and sported a hot pink halter top, faded blue jeans, and a pair of golden sandals. Must have been her favorite as they were the same she'd worn with her fae costume. Her brown hair hung down to her hips in satiny curls now, but the clips with the sapphires still pulled the strands out of her face.

Alicia could see how Deveron could be smitten with the

beautiful fae.

She smiled at Cassie, ignoring Alicia and said, "Micala and Deveron sent me to keep you company. Deveron said he'd left enough money that I could have lunch on him also. I sure am famished." She turned to Alicia and smiled, but the look wasn't entirely friendly. "Aren't you?"

* * *

Deveron stood before his mother as she gave him one of her you'd-better-mind-me looks.

She wore her royal gowns of deep purple with an embroidered golden sash draped diagonally across her body. She only wore the sash when she administered court. He imagined he'd pulled her away from her duties to dispense justice in the fae realm.

Which meant she was peeved with him.

"I understand you have been entertaining two female humans at a beach resort." Her voice sounded cold and irritated.

What he wanted to know was who ratted on him?

"It doesn't matter how I know, but that I do." She couldn't read minds, but she came awfully close to it. "What did I tell you, Deveron?"

Don't mess with the humans. But the fae traditionally played games with them. Why stop what had been a satisfying ritual for many millennia?

Should he tell her he had a most important mission? Discover how the human could see them? Or would his mother put someone else in charge of the investigation?

Most likely.

But if she caught him having anything further to do with the human girl, his mother might go through with her threat to turn him into a human for a time. That would end his desire to be with them.

That's what she'd said anyway.

"Yes, my lady mother," Deveron acquiesced.

"I mean it, Deveron."

He bowed his head. "I understand." But he had no plan to give in to his mother...not when the girl needed to be thoroughly investigated.

And he had every intention of doing the job.

Did others like her exist? It could lead to the downfall of their people, couldn't it?

If nothing more, it definitely put a crimp in his playing tricks on the humans when one knew what he was. But it was a challenge he couldn't resist.

"I must return to court, but I have an important errand for you to handle," his mother said.

The old errand-to-run trick that would keep him from returning to the beach resort.

Well, whatever it was, he'd either get someone else to handle it, or he'd take care of it quickly.

"Yes, my lady mother. What is the task you wish me to accomplish?"

She smiled and the look was pure wickedness.

Definitely, not good.

CHAPTER 4

The female faery took Deveron's seat at the Mexican restaurant, turned to Cassie and said, "I'm Ritasia. Deveron is my brother."

Alicia quickly closed her gaping mouth. So the faery wasn't Deveron's girlfriend, but his sister, to take up where he left off.

"I'm Cassie and that's Alicia," Cassie offered. "Are Micala and Deveron coming back soon?"

Ritasia shook her head. "I'm afraid not."

"That's too bad." Alicia hoped the tone of her voice didn't give away the fact she was tremendously pleased. She turned as their waitress carried another platter full of fajitas to their table.

Ritasia smiled. "I caught the waitress and she threw my order on."

"Good." Cassie piled guacamole, sour cream, beef and peppers on top of a tortilla. "Especially since you are so famished."

Alicia rolled her eyes. Cassie never met a stranger. She acted as though she'd known the fae forever.

Then the man behind them complained to the waitress, "How come she got her meal before I did? I ordered the same thing twenty minutes ago."

Ritasia winked at Alicia.

Had the mischievous fae intercepted the man's fajita order?

Ritasia folded her stuffed tortilla into an envelope, then said to Alicia, "It must be nice to have a girlfriend here with you. Being with my brother and his...friend isn't the same as being with a girlfriend."

"Why did you come then?" Alicia asked.

"To keep an eye on my brother. Why else?" Ritasia smiled broadly.

"He seems old enough to be on his own." Alicia stabbed her fork into a slice of beef, then added it to her tortilla. She didn't feel that the sister fae was watching out for her brother.

Rather, Ritasia intended to trifle with the humans now that he was gone.

* * *

Deveron paced across the green marble floor of the castle keep of Venicia. Escorting the Venician princess, Lorelei, to her coming out on her sixteenth birthday, wasn't what he had in mind to do. But no matter how hard he'd tried to get his mother to reconsider, she wouldn't. He wondered then if she had some ulterior motive. He was to escort the girl wherever and whenever she wanted for a whole lousy week!

Micala watched him for some time, then finally took a ragged breath. "My lord, shouldn't you have told Queen Irenis why you wanted to see the human girl further?"

"She would have taken perverse pleasure in having someone else discover the girl's identity and why she can see us like she can."

Micala ran his hands over his satin tunic. "I did some research in our ancient archives before we came here and found some interesting material I'd never known before."

"Oh?"

"Over a thousand years ago, a fae mated with a human woman. Their offspring had similar abilities to this girl."

Deveron stared at him, then sat down hard on a wooden bench. "And?"

"The fae was forced to give up the human and the reigning queen ordered the offspring destroyed."

"What if they weren't all killed? What if Alicia is the descendent of one of these?" Deveron rubbed his chin. "Or what if other fae have fathered these...these half-immortals?"

"It's possible. I believe the recorded case had six children. Anyway, I couldn't find anything more in the archives. Of, course this is mainly about our own fae. There might be some from the other realms who have done the same thing. Though it is forbidden for any fae to attach themselves to a human."

Deveron's eyes widened, the thought totally disconcerting. "She could be from another fae house?"

"That's what I was thinking."

Deveron stood, then began to pace. "Another royal house."

"Not a royal house, exactly, but what about another fae kingdom, my lord?"

"Yes, yes." Deveron motioned Micala to be quiet. "That's what I meant. We have to return at once. I must know who her parents were."

"But if neither are fae—"

"We must find out her lineage. We must!"

"What must you do?" Princess Lorelei asked, her red curls pulled tight against her head, making her thin face appear tortured, though she managed a smile. She fingered the golden medallion at her throat embossed with the gargoyle.

He forced a small smile to placate her, though he had no desire to play nursemaid to a sixteen-year-old princess who had plenty of suitors, any of whom would leap at the chance to serve in his capacity. Suddenly, he looked over at Micala. His mother hadn't intended for Deveron to be the princess's suitor, had she?

He groaned deep inside. Sure she would. As unreasonable as she could be. "I'm sorry, Princess Lorelei, but I'm afraid an urgent matter at Denkar has need of my immediate attention. Please forgive me. I will return as soon as possible."

He bowed low and kissed her hand. Then he tilted his head up and looked at Micala who bowed to the princess.

Before she could utter a word, her eyes grew wide with

28

astonishment, and he and Micala returned to the Mexican restaurant on South Padre Island, hopeful that the fae-spy would still be eating her lunch.

But when they walked into the main dining area, they found another couple sitting at the table.

Deveron cursed under his breath. "Come, we'll return to their hotel. Perhaps they're there."

"What about Princess Lorelei, my lord? Surely you realize she'll report this to her parents, and even if she doesn't, they'll know you're not there to escort her anywhere. Word will get back to your mother and then—"

"Yes, well I told the princess I would return soon, and I meant it. All we have to do is find Alicia and force the truth from her."

"The lady doesn't seem to be the kind of girl who bows to pressure easily."

"She will. Believe me, she will."

"You are forbidden from using faery magic on a human, my lord."

Deveron shook his head. "I will use whatever means necessary to find out what fae line she descends from before my mother learns of it."

They walked into the men's room and as there was no one there, they both vanished.

Deveron and Micala ended up at the hotel and remained invisible outside Alicia and Cassie's hotel room door. With no one about, Deveron knocked on the door.

When there was no answer, he transferred himself inside the room. Micala followed. Neither of the girls was there.

Deveron sucked in his breath with annoyance. "Where would they have gone?"

Micala pointed at the carpeted floor. "Your sister's been here."

Deveron studied the almost imperceptible trail of fae dust, the signature as unique to faeries as a fingerprint was to humans.

"She must have discovered Alicia was fae-knowing."

"Or she wished to play tricks on the girls as you had intended."

"Where would they have gone?" Deveron asked again. His neck muscles tightened with annoyance. What was his sister up to?

"Shopping?" Micala suggested. "Human females seem to spend an inordinate amount of time shopping."

"We don't even know what kind of a conveyance they own."

Voices approached the room and Deveron folded his arms, stood fast and stared at the door.

"Shouldn't we leave?" Micala asked.

"No. I will find out who she is and—"

The lock clicked open and the door opened.

A brown-skinned maid entered the room with a fresh load of towels.

Deveron released an exasperated breath. "Come. Let's check out the shopping areas."

"We might pick up Princess Ritasia's trail along the way."

"If it hasn't gone cold by now. But you're right. Let's go."

Deveron and Micala visited every beach resort T-shirt and post card shop...all the typical souvenir shops. Then they surveyed the classier boutiques. They found not a sign of either the humans or his sister.

"Do you think maybe they returned home? Maybe they were leaving today. Or perhaps Alicia worried about you having discovered her secret, and she convinced her friend they should return home."

Disagreeably, Deveron had to consider that option. "She may very well know that the fae killed people like her in the past."

"We may still do so, my lord. Your mother may have the girl eliminated if she feels Alicia is a threat to our people."

"Then we must find her first."

Micala's brow furrowed into a deep frown. "Not to protect her, surely."

Deveron scowled. "What do you take me for? Protection of the fae kind is tantamount in any situation." Then he ground his teeth as he considered another matter. Princess Lorelei. "You don't think my mother intended for me to court the Venician princess, do you?"

"She wishes an alliance with their people, yes. It's either you wed Princess Lorelei or your sister takes the princess's older brother for her mate."

"Ritasia can have the Venician prince. I won't wed Lorelei. She's a mouse." What he wouldn't have given for a princess who had Alicia's spunkiness. The nerve of the girl to douse him with sodas. And yet, just that boldness was what he liked in a woman. He shook his head to think his thoughts would even go there. No way would he risk all to become interested in a human.

"We missed that card shop over there, my lord," Micala suddenly said.

They transferred themselves to the sidewalk outside of the shop but before they walked inside, Micala pointed at the concrete. A sparkle of luminescent sea green faery dust—Ritasia's—caught their attention. The two followed it to a movie theater.

Deveron smiled. "I believe we have found our quarry."

They appeared inside the building, then followed the trail to the third door on the right. Micala opened the door for Deveron, then the two proceeded to follow the dust, shimmering like a trail of tiny Christmas lights on a dark night. They both made themselves visible, then followed the trail up the stairs.

Due to the early afternoon hour and the fact the feature had been playing for a week and a half already, the theater was half empty. Both he and Micala spied Ritasia and the two human females sitting dead center in a row of seats, otherwise unoccupied by other humans.

Despite the seriousness of the feature as a car chase scene screeched across the screen, Ritasia and Alicia saw Deveron and Micala at once.

Ritasia shook her head at him.

He could have done the same with her. He stalked down the aisle toward them.

Cassie, finally noticing Micala and Deveron, smiled with enthusiasm.

Micala went around the other way to sit beside Cassie.

Deveron said to Ritasia so he could sit next to Alicia, "Move over."

"You're always so diplomatic when you want your way." Ritasia scooted over to free up the seat next to Alicia.

He took the seat and looked at Alicia. She ignored him. He smiled. It wouldn't work.

Alicia folded her arms.

Deveron reached over and took her hand in his and held tight. "Tell me who your parents are, or I can't protect you." Not that he was certain he could anyway, or that he would want to.

She glared at him and tried to pull her hand away. But when she'd couldn't, she turned her attention to the movie and pretended he didn't exist.

Fae females were always ready to please him, being he was a prince. And human females were intrigued by his looks and actions. The fact the fae-knower wouldn't be charmed by him intrigued him to no end.

"Do you know how powerful fae magic can be?" he whispered in her ear. He breathed in her peach scent and realized at once she had a slightly different fragrance than humans. Almost like...

He shook his head, ignoring the notion that flitted across his mind. "And do you realize no matter how much you try, you can't ever resist me?"

Alicia shuddered. Not because she was afraid of the dark fae, but because he tickled her ear with his warm breath.

"What do you know about us?" he asked, as one dark brow rose in a cocky manner.

"That you're evil." Alicia tilted her chin up as she waited for his response.

At first he just stared at her.

Then his lips curved up, every bit as dangerously as she knew he was. "All the more reason to tell me why you can see and hear us in our other state, before I resort to dark fae techniques."

CHAPTER 5

Alicia noticed then that Ritasia strained to hear their conversation in the movie theater as the car chase continued across the screen. From the frown wrinkling Ritasia's brow, Alicia assumed the fae wasn't getting the gist of her conversation with Deveron.

Alicia sighed heavily. She had no idea what the dark fae could do to her as her father had only mentioned that humans who could see them would be terminated. Now she wished she could meet him, if only so that she could talk to him about her peculiarity and what to do in the situation she now found herself in.

She continued to watch the film, though she didn't see anything but the flash of headlights, balls of fire, and the sparks streaking across the screen as metal ground against metal. Her concentration remained on the fae who held her hand, possessively, heating her thoroughly. But more than that, she knew he studied her with the same kind of wolfish bemused expression. And that's what distracted her something fierce.

He leaned over and whispered, "I've never had any girl, fae or human, act so spitefully toward me. Whatever had I done to deserve wearing the ice cold drinks on my bare chest?"

She smiled, but wouldn't look at him. His dark eyes were deadly entrancing, charming, lulling her into a false sense of desire. He didn't want her. He wanted her to beg for mercy before he had her killed. Or did the job himself.

He added, "It took every bit of resolve for me not to flinch when the icy sodas hit my chest."

Alicia's smile broadened. So he wasn't as tough as he acted. She could just imagine him trying to pretend not to be unsettled by the ice hitting his sun-warmed skin for the human girl's benefit. Though she wondered why he'd be so honest about it with her now. Did he think if he gave up a secret, she would, too?

No way would she tell him who her father was. Not that she knew anyway. Her mother had kept her maiden name so the fae wouldn't ever be able to learn Alicia's father's name. And Alicia only knew her father's first name...

Suddenly golden-haired fae, six of them, dressed in navy blue tunics and dark brown trousers appeared at the bottom of the stairs. For a moment, they looked at the carpeted floor, then turned their attention to Deveron and the rest of his party. At once, the six male fae tromped up the stairs to Alicia's aisle. From their grim expressions, they looked like they had a formidable mission. Were they coming to arrest her?

Instantly, her stomach muscles tightened. Deveron's hand grasped hers more firmly also. Was he protecting her? Or keeping her there so she could be taken prisoner?

He was a dark fae. He wouldn't be helping her. She tried to free her hand from his steel grasp.

"You're in trouble now if the royal guards are coming for you," Ritasia warned.

Alicia knew it. She was a dead woman.

Deveron cursed under his breath, then leaned over and kissed Alicia's lips. Before she could react, shove him away, enjoy his attention, slip out of his reach, or kiss him back, her head began to swim in circles around and around, faster and faster as if she was riding a spinning top at an amusement park. Everything swirled into the dim light of the theater to a much darker void.

Could a dark fae's kiss disorient her that much?

She tried to concentrate on him, on the feel of his warm lips pressing with such passion against hers, on his hand that gripped hers for dear life. Then the swirling slowed down. The dark gave into light. The smell of buttered popcorn turned into the fragrance of fresh grass. No longer was she sitting upright in a theater chair, but she reclined on a bed of soft, tall grass.

Her eyes began to focus on her new surroundings.

Too dizzy, she couldn't sit up. She tried to open her mouth to speak as Deveron leaned over her, watching her, not saying a word. Her stomach's queasiness began to settle.

For what seemed like an eternity, she attempted to focus on him, on the dazzling blue sky above, and the puffs of white clouds that she could make out.

Birds chattered in a forest—a forest?—just a few feet away. There were no forests on South Padre Island.

She closed her eyes and tried to make sense of what had just happened. She was watching a suspense thriller with Cassie and Ritasia, then suddenly, Deveron and Micala arrived. And then...and then a gap in her memory prevented her from remembering what else.

She looked at Deveron's lips. They curved in a naughty grin. He'd kissed her. But no. Something before that. What had happened? Think, Alicia, think.

Somehow she figured knowing what had happened before the kiss would prove tantamount to her survival. But as much as she attempted to remember, she couldn't.

He leaned over further and took her hand in his and touched his lips to hers.

She should object. Shouldn't she? He was a dark fae and she was...she was...was she a dark fae, too? She couldn't remember. Why couldn't she remember?

His name was Deveron and he was...he was kissing her—again.

She tangled her fingers in his dark brown, shoulder length hair, the rich color shimmering in the warm sunlight. The gold around his eyes sparkled with an intensity she hadn't remembered before. Then they closed as he deepened his kiss.

"Alicia," he mouthed against her lips, uttered with such longing and desire, she knew he loved her.

Her brow furrowed for a moment. Didn't he?

He kissed her eyes, one with profound reverence, then the other. He moved to her cheeks, doing both of them the honor next. And then her lips again. And she succumbed. No one had ever kissed her with such tenderness, such finesse, such passion. She was in love. Had to be.

Male voices spoken some distance away garnered their attention. Alicia parted her lips to speak, but Deveron covered them with his again. She gave into his loving touch, but then the swirling began all over.

She groaned as her world shifted from golden light and sweet smelling grass to rotating dark and the only scent, Deveron. His subtle spicy fae fragrance drew her under his spell.

When dark faded to light and she managed to focus on her new surroundings, she realized to her horror, she was laying beneath Deveron in a pale blue velvet bed surrounded by the same colored curtains that shrouded them in secrecy. A human girl pinned to a very comfortable bed by her enemy.

She opened her mouth to object, but Deveron shook his head at her and clamped his hand over her lips to keep her quiet.

"Stay here, while I get something for you to wear," he whispered in warning. "Do not, whatever you do, leave the bed. Neither of us can afford any of the other Denkar fae catching you here."

"Where are we?" Though she suspected it was his bed—his bedroom—or he would not have been so bold to bring her here.

"My bedchambers at Castle Donao, the kingdom of Denkar."

Why in heaven's name did he bring her here of all places? In the middle of the spider's web where the black widow of them all would devour her in one fell swoop?

A chill trickled down her spine. "Deveron, why did you bring me here?" As if she didn't know. To play with her as he would with any human girl. And then when it wasn't safe or fun anymore, give her up to the powers to be.

He grasped her hand. "To keep you safe. To protect you. I promise that's my only intention."

She scowled at him. "A promise from an evil dark fae?"

He lips twitched upward slightly. "You'll have to trust me."

She gasped as she thought of Cassie. "Cassie! What of Cassie?"

"Micala will take good care of her."

She frowned at him.

A slow smile curved his lips. "He's not a dark fae, or I should say...not evil like me. He won't allow any harm to come to her."

"But what about me? I mean, she'll be worried that I disappeared...that I—"

"He's made sure she only thinks he's been with her. As far as she knows, she's alone on this trip, and she and he will share some fun times together, nothing more."

"Fun times?"

"Pleasant...nothing unseemingly."

Why didn't she believe him? Because he was a dark fae...that's why. "Why did you bring me *here*?" she asked again. "You had *no* reason to."

"The royal guard was after us."

"Us?"

"I'm supposed to be elsewhere. But if they had learned or were to learn what you're capable of..." He shook his head. "I didn't want to have to worry about your well-being. You'll be safer with me."

She glowered at him with her most evil, narrow-eyed glare. "It's because of you that I'm in this mess."

He smiled at her words. But he hesitated to leave her. "Are you going to be all right?"

"Right. I happen to be in the wicked lair of the dark fae."

His dark brows knit together in a frown. He whispered in her ear. "Stay put and I will return shortly."

Alicia nodded, but she wouldn't release his hand.

His lips curved up again, only this time his eyes warmed and twinkled with a strange mixture of delight and intrigue. "Would you like for me to give you a goodbye kiss?"

She released his hand at once.

"I should world jump with you more often. It makes you more...compliant."

She slapped his chest and whispered, "Go and hurry back. Then you can...why do I need to change clothes?"

"To blend in with the other blond-haired fae."

"Why would I need to do that? I mean, why can't you return me to—"

"You are going to stay close by my side. End of discussion."

She scowled at him, not caring for his superior male attitude.

He grinned at her, kissed her lips, nipping the bottom one, and when she touched her tongue to his to show him he wasn't so much in charge, he groaned. "Later, faery princess."

Faery princess. She was a human who was in a whole lot of trouble.

And then he vanished.

All at once her skin erupted in goose flesh. Alone in unfamiliar surroundings a sudden sense of disquiet filled her. What if he didn't return? What if she got caught in his bed?

She sniffed at the bed linens. They smelled like Deveron. And then the realization sank in that she was indeed in his bed.

Great! If his parents should catch her here of all places, she'd be dead meat.

She scrambled through the bed curtains and meant to stand on the floor, but as soon as her feet touched the woven rug, she collapsed to her knees. Her head swam with dizziness as her stomach grew nauseous.

Then women's voices grew close to the room, and Alicia's heartbeat quickened as she grabbed for the bed curtains.

CHAPTER 6

"I swear I was with him one moment and the next, he was gone," a woman said somewhere outside Deveron's room as Alicia fumbled with the bed curtains.

Was Ritasia the one who was speaking?

"If you are hiding anything concerning this matter, it will not go easy for either you or your brother," a woman warned. Her voice sounded older and concerned.

"I had nothing to do with his disappearance," Ritasia insisted. Her voice grew closer to the bedroom door as her footsteps padded outside the room. "Why should I wish to get into trouble for my brother's folly?"

The curved brass handle on the door began to twist down. Alicia grappled with the bed curtains, trying to find the entrance into the bed as her heart sped up its pace and a trickle of perspiration dribbled between her breasts.

Work legs, work, she scolded them silently as her whole body seemed to be moving in perpetually slow motion.

"Because, Princess Ritasia, you are like two dark kernels on an ear of corn, clinging side by side. The queen knows you often help your brother out of predicaments he gets himself into. Only this time it's much too serious. Either your brother weds the Venician princess Lorelei, or you wed her brother. That's what your mother just announced one of you would do. Strife in the kingdoms and such. The Denkar royalty wish an alliance with the Venicians, too."

"I won't. Deveron will have to marry Lorelei."

Ritasia peeked through Deveron's bed curtains as if afraid of what she'd find.

Alicia bolted out the other side. And fell on the floor. What was wrong with her fool legs? Her bones had turned to rubber.

"What was that thump?" the woman asked.

Footsteps hurried toward the other side of the bed. The side where Alicia sat on the floor, totally shaken. She crawled under the bed.

"Nothing," Ritasia said, quickly, worry evident in her voice. "See? Nothing. Must have been something that fell in the bedchambers next to Deveron's."

Alicia watched as their golden sandaled feet walked away from the bed.

"Why don't you continue your search, Lady Manantos? I'll wait here a while, just in case my dear brother returns anytime soon."

"You will not attempt to aid him?"

"Hmpf. Why should I? What does he ever do for me, but give me grief?"

"True enough. However, you have done so before."

The door closed and then footsteps hurried back to the bed. Before Alicia could scurry out from under the bed in the opposite direction, Ritasia peered underneath the bed skirt. She grinned. "This is too funny. Whatever are you doing in here?"

"Hiding." Though Alicia assumed it was obvious what she was doing sprawled out under Deveron's bed.

Ritasia reached her hand out to her. "Come. If anyone else searches for you here, I can take you safely to my own bedchambers. For now, I can freely move about the castle. Though I don't know how long before my mother sets the guard on me." Ritasia helped pull Alicia out from under the bed. "Get back in his bed. Where has he gone to anyway?"

"To get some clothes for me to wear, he said."

"To get some of *my* clothes." Ritasia frowned, then her face brightened. "Can't be helped. Whatever does he hope to pass you off as?"

"A fae."

Ritasia giggled and touched a lock of Alicia's blond hair. "Well, yes I suppose so."

"I've seen blond-haired fae with Deveron. Micala is one even." Alicia tried to stand, but closed her eyes as a wave of dizziness washed over her.

"Oh," Ritasia said. "You're not used to fae travel." She helped Alicia onto the massive mattress that spanned the width of two king-sized beds shoved together. Why would Deveron need one that large?

Ritasia climbed onto the mattress and shut the curtains.

"Thanks for telling the other lady I was not here."

Ritasia smiled. "I couldn't. What fun would there be in that? But as to your remark about the blond-haired fae, well, except for Micala and a few others, I should amend. Most are not of the royal house of Denkar. They serve us and have for many millennia. If any of the Denkar fae found you to be in Deveron's company, you would be suspect at once. Everyone knows who the royals are. He doesn't associate with the female blond-haired fae. So he must be planning something else. Though nothing comes to mind." Ritasia patted Alicia's hand. "Lie down. Get your strength back. I'm sure Deveron plans to transport you again. Repeated transportation the fae way for one who is not accustomed to it, can be incapacitating at the very least."

"How would you know?" Alicia asked as she took Ritasia's advice and laid her head against the soft down pillow.

"When we haven't jumped from place to place for a while, even the Denkar can become disoriented. Deveron does it so often, he never does. But I don't transport as frequently as he does."

"Why don't you marry the Venician prince?"

Ritasia's eyes widened. "How would you know...oh, you

overheard my lady-in-waiting's conversation with me. Not only do I not love the conceited Prince Phillinois, I can't stand him."

Before Alicia could speak further to Ritasia about the prince, Deveron appeared in front of her on the mattress.

He turned and scowled at Ritasia.

She smiled back at him and raised her brows.

"What in curses are you doing here?"

Ritasia ignored his words. Her gaze shifted to the garments Deveron had taken from her room. "You could have asked my permission."

"How could I when you were not in your chambers but in mine? Whoever gave you permission to enter mine anyway?"

"Me, after I was grilled thoroughly about your vanishing with Alicia. Where do you intend to take her next?"

"Change," he said to Alicia. Then he climbed off the bed and Ritasia joined him, pulling the curtains closed again.

Alicia removed her shirt and then her sandals and jeans. She pulled the purple satin gown over her head while wispy sheers of the same color of purple attached to the gown floated down to the mattress. Now she felt like a faery princess.

"I wouldn't tell you my plans," Deveron said to Ritasia.

"I've already kept your secret."

"She did," Alicia said from behind the bed curtains. She figured they needed all of the alliances they could get. Though on the other hand, she wasn't sure she could trust either of them completely.

"I have to return to fulfill my duties escorting Princess Lorelei," Deveron said.

Ritasia laughed. "But what about Alicia? Surely you don't intend for me to attempt to hide her here."

"She will be our dear cousin…a sixth removed and will accompany me."

"But I don't have dark hair." Alicia pulled on a sandal.

"Some of our distant cousins are blond," Deveron remarked. "Most don't live here. Aren't you dressed yet?"

42

"I feel as though I'm moving in slow motion."

"From transporting her," Ritasia reminded him.

"Oh."

Alicia pulled the curtain aside.

Deveron considered the way her gowns shimmered over her form. His expression indicated deepest admiration. Did he prefer her wearing the dress of the fae? It appeared so. But she reminded herself he was her enemy as much as she wished in an instant of madness that he wasn't.

Ritasia socked him in the shoulder. "She needs some of my clips for her hair, if you're going to pass her off as one of the Denkar fae of the minor royal branches. And pull in your tongue. It's dragging the floor."

He frowned at Ritasia.

She shook her head and vanished.

Alicia sat on the edge of the bed, not trusting her legs to hold her if she stood.

His lips curved up in that same mischievous way he had before that totally disarmed and warmed her throughout.

"You know, you have the most charming smile," she said.

"It's one of my most gifted dark fae qualities."

"And you're terribly conceited."

He grinned. "Now there's my Alicia. I thought I'd lost you."

She made an annoyed face at him.

He chuckled under his breath.

Ritasia appeared next to him. She reached over and fastened golden clips decorated in sparkling amethysts to Alicia's hair.

"Thank you, Ritasia. I will always be in your debt."

"Yes, you will be," the girl said, and Alicia was afraid that didn't bode well.

"Come, we must go, Alicia, before we're discovered here," Deveron said, pulling her up from the bed.

"Wait." Ritasia slipped a gold medallion, dangling from a gold chain, over Alicia's head. "Now you are officially a sixth cousin of the dark fae of the kingdom of Neferon."

Alicia glanced down at the medallion that pictured an embossed turtle. "Turtle?"

"They live by the sea and revere the power and steadfastness of the giant sea turtle," Deveron said.

"Ah." It just didn't seem half as proud and strong as the lion, the Denkar's symbol. Alicia took Ritasia's hands and leaned over and kissed her cheek. "Thank you, Ritasia. I'll never forget this."

Ritasia's eyes widened and her lips parted. Then she turned to Deveron who grinned.

He said, "You've made my sister speechless, which believe me, rarely happens."

He took Alicia's hand and pulled her close. So close she could feel his breath on her cheek. And then he kissed her lips again.

She thought she heard Ritasia say, "So that's how you've done it."

And the room faded to black.

CHAPTER 7

When light replaced the dark, Alicia breathed in the delightful fragrance of lilacs dripping in purple grape clusters over sandstone walls. And red roses gathered at their base. Grape hyacinths nestled at their feet making the place smell like a bit of fairyland.

It *was* a fairyland. The Venician kingdom of fae.

"Venicia," Deveron said, holding her arms to steady her. He moved her to a stone bench and sat her down. "I'm to escort Princess Lorelei at her whim to wherever she wishes to go, but I will have to take you, too, as frail as you are. You need your cousin's assistance in your delicate condition."

She rolled her eyes. Though she did feel slightly incapacitated with fae travel again. Not as bad this time. Was she adjusting to it?

He smiled. "Despite how becoming you look in Ritasia's gowns, your cheeks are as white as the clouds above. You appear ready to faint."

"I'm not faint," she said, firmly. Though if she stood…

Footsteps closing in on them caught their attention, and they turned to see who approached.

A blond-haired male, tall and thin, wearing a highly embroidered dark blue tunic, bowed low to Deveron. "My lord. Princess Lorelei has been unduly concerned that you left so all of a sudden." The elder man looked at Alicia with disdain, then turned his attention again to Deveron. "Have you returned to take over your duties where she's concerned?"

"Yes, Lord Carsonet. But my cousin, Princess Alicia, needs my attention as well."

The man frowned. "Surely you do not mean to escort Princess Lorelei while you…" He glanced at Alicia. "Why does Queen Irenis not have someone else look after Princess Alicia? A physician perhaps? She looks unwell."

She narrowed her eyes at him. This man said it in such a hateful manner, her temperature elevated a whole ten degrees. Her cheeks must have flushed red as hot as they felt.

"I will be fine after a bit," she said.

"A week," Deveron amended.

She glared at him. How was she to look sickly for a whole week?

"The whole week you will be here with Princess Lorelei?" Lord Carsonet said, his voice raised in disbelief.

"Do you have some trouble with this?" Deveron folded his arms and pinned him with a glare. He didn't appear to be a man to be trifled with.

"No, Prince Deveron. I will inform the princess you are here. I'm sure she would delight in your walking her in the gardens. They are a great pleasure to her." The man bowed, then turned and hastened back to the courtyard.

Alicia took a deep breath, not liking the role she had to play now. How could she pull off being a fae? "He sounded displeased, Deveron."

"He is the castle steward. But he has no business telling me how I am to handle my affairs."

"If the princess walks in the garden with you, I can sit here and enjoy the fragrance of the flowers."

"No. If you cannot walk, we'll find something you can do. I won't leave you behind."

She rubbed her temple, the dizziness fading from there. "Do you think someone here will realize I'm not who I say I am?"

"I wouldn't dare let my guard down."

She took a deep breath, not understanding their fae logic. "Why didn't you just return me home?"

"They would have found you."

"Who?"

He crouched at her knees and took her hands in his. "The Denkar royal guard."

"But won't they find me here sooner? I mean, what if someone discovers I can't move like you do. That I can't become invisible to humans."

"Not all fae transport themselves like that. Some hate the side effects too much. And if you are among fae, you would have no need to become invisible. The fae could see you anyway. It's only among the humans that we become invisible."

"And on occasion, visible."

He smiled.

"Why do you care what happens to me?" The notion had plagued her ever since he kissed her the first time. Had he unduly influenced her with dark fae magic? Bound her under his spell?

Deveron stared at her for a moment, then his lips turned up slowly. "Truthfully?"

Could she handle the truth in her delicate condition? She nearly laughed out loud at herself. She nodded.

"No one has ever doused me with ice cold drinks before. There has to be an appropriate payback. You're mine until I think of an adequate revenge." His dark brown eyes sparkled with delight.

"You're kidding right?"

His smile broadened. "Ask Ritasia. I don't get angry, Alicia. I get even. Another dark fae quality."

"You already got your revenge when you took me prisoner."

"You're my guest, my faery princess. Until I say otherwise."

"Amuse yourself with the human a while longer?"

"Precisely. As long as you continue to intrigue me, you're mine. Another dark fae quality—extreme possessiveness. Cannot be helped."

Before she could tell him just what she thought of his dark fae qualities, royal blue gowns, sparkling in the sunlight, caught her eye. And then she saw the thin-faced girl, whose red hair was pulled so severely back, it made Alicia's temple throb...or maybe it was the fae travel that had unsettled her so.

Deveron released Alicia's hands and stood.

The girl's catlike green eyes glared at Alicia. The girl obviously didn't care for the intrusion. She crossed the courtyard with two ladies in tow. Her medieval chaperones? Maybe they thought Deveron would kiss Lorelei the way he'd kissed Alicia and that was forbidden. She swallowed hard. Yeah, the way the prince had kissed her should be forbidden. She looked at his lips that had thinned into a straight line as he watched Lorelei approach.

The thought he'd even want to kiss the girl—

"I'm so pleased you have returned, Deveron." The girl took his hands in hers and kissed each of his cheeks.

If her blood could turn green with envy, Alicia's just did. She wondered, though, why she was jealous. She couldn't be resentful of a dark fae who had the hots for another fae.

Deveron greeted Lorelei in the same manner, then grinned at Alicia, who had to be wearing a Texas-sized scowl.

Deveron motioned to Alicia. "Princess Lorelei, meet my cousin, Princess Alicia."

"From Neferon?" Lorelei asked, avoiding looking at Alicia.

"Yes."

"I thought so." She ran her hand over Deveron's hair. "I didn't think anyone in your direct line had light hair."

"A very few." He raised his brows at the tenderness the Venician princess showed him, and Alicia assumed this was a new side to Lorelei he'd never seen before.

Was she showing her female possessiveness? If Alicia hadn't been pretending to be Deveron's distant cousin, she'd have put some moves on Deveron to outdo the snooty redhead. Well, not because Alicia felt anything for him, but she knew he wanted out of the relationship with Lorelei, and she wouldn't have minded helping, just a little.

But of course if Alicia did anything like that, she was certain she'd put herself in more danger. Cool it, Alicia. Be the weak, indisposed nobody and blend into the background like a shy violet tucked beneath a shrub full of blooming roses.

Shy violet her foot. She'd never be able to play that role.

Alicia reached out to Deveron and yanked at the bottom edge of his tunic. "Isn't he a sweetheart?"

He couldn't have grinned any bigger nor could Lorelei have given her a more demonic look. Oh well, nobody could say humans didn't have their own devilish moments to want to even up the score.

"Your cousin can remain behind here to rest as my steward said she is unwell. One of my ladies can see to her."

"I'm to keep an eye on her at all times," Deveron said.

"Oh? Even when she beds down for the night?" Lorelei smiled. "I'm teasing of course."

Right.

Wouldn't Lorelei like to know how Alicia had been with him in his bed already, as innocent as it was?

But before an issue could be made of whether they would take a walk with or without the pretend princess, Ritasia appeared.

"Here you are," Ritasia said to Deveron and Alicia. She smiled. "What are we doing?"

Lorelei stiffened her back.

Ritasia winked at Alicia. Evidently, Ritasia didn't get along with Lorelei any more than Ritasia did with the princess's brother.

Lorelei quickly said, "Deveron is taking me for a walk. Since you arrived at such an opportune time, perhaps you could stay with your cousin and watch over her instead."

Deveron took a deep breath of exasperation. Alicia imagined he was sorely vexed with his sister's intrusion. But truthfully, Alicia felt it would be best for all concerned, for the moment.

"I can," Ritasia said.

Lorelei took Deveron's arm. "Later, ladies." The two maids followed them along the stone path, keeping a respectful distance.

When they disappeared down the path, Ritasia sat next to Alicia on the stone bench. "They were still searching for you and Deveron at the castle, having found traces of his recent faery dust trail in his room. But then word reached us that he was taking his duties concerning Lorelei to heart and that was the end of the concern. For the most part."

"For the most part?"

"You've caused quite a stir, Alicia. Deveron has never transported a human girl anywhere before. And the rumor you can see the fae when we're invisible has reached my mother. The search continues for you, but not in the Denkar kingdom."

"They'll assume I'm with Deveron. Don't you think?"

"Maybe. Though I'm sure no one wants to upset Lorelei so they wouldn't want to make a scene in attempting to apprehend you here. Or they may believe he wouldn't risk offending Lorelei and bring you here. In any event, they are searching other kingdoms at the moment. Though not all will be receptive to our questioning."

"And Cassie?"

"She is fine. Micala is a good fae. A perfect gentleman."

Alicia looked in the direction Deveron had taken. "Does he always get even?"

Ritasia laughed. "You bet. Why?"

Alicia shook her head.

Ritasia's brown eyes sparkled with interest. "You will have to tell me someday what prompted that question." She ran her hands over her emerald green gowns. "I have to know who your parents are."

But Alicia knew Ritasia meant she wished to know who Alicia's fae parent was. Alicia felt she had to know, too, if she was going to survive this hunt for her. She felt that Ritasia might be able to help her find her father. But if Alicia found him, would he protect her? Or pretend the half human/half fae wasn't his daughter? She stamped down the sorrowful feelings that rose up deep inside her. She shouldn't care. She couldn't. Survival was all that was important for now.

"I never knew my father's name."

"Then he's the fae."

"He wrote in a journal about fae ways. About several of the kingdoms."

"About the Denkar?"

Alicia nodded.

"Some of the other kingdoms wrote some awful things about us. But in history you'll find no society is above doing wrong at some time or another."

"Your people destroyed my kind."

"Fae-knowers?" Ritasia swallowed hard. "Yes."

"And your mother would have me put to death if she knew the truth about me."

"We don't know that," Ritasia said, defending her mother.

"You think she wouldn't?"

"If you endangered our kind…" She let her words trail off. "Or she may keep you prisoner. On the other hand she will not like it that Deveron is so infatuated with you."

"As a human plaything. To get even with me."

Ritasia smiled. "Pray tell what did you do to him?"

CHAPTER 8

Alicia wouldn't tell Ritasia what she had done to Deveron to solicit his promise he'd get even with her, though she was amused his sister would be so intrigued.

"I swear whatever it is that you have done, you have gotten him wrapped tightly around your finger. You pull the string, and he'll come running," Ritasia said.

"Nonsense. He's a dark fae. He has no interest in a human."

"But you're not exactly all human, are you? Maybe that's what intrigues him most about you."

"My father must have been fae."

"Yes. Did he stay with your mother?"

"Only until I was five." No matter how many times she told herself she didn't care, she did. Even now her heart felt like a block of cement, and her eyes grew tearful.

Ritasia nodded. "It would be difficult to ignore his own kind for very long. Or maybe..." She rubbed her hands, seemingly deep in thought as she squinted her eyes and stared at the ground.

"What?"

Ritasia faced Alicia. "Maybe, he worried for you and your mother's safety. Maybe he abandoned you to keep his kind from learning about you."

Deep down, Alicia had always resented her father for leaving her mother and her. But what if he did it to protect them from the vindictiveness of the fae? Then he was a hero, not a villain. He'd left the ones he'd loved to protect them.

"Maybe you're right." She hoped Ritasia was. And now she was truly determined to locate her father.

"Sure," Ritasia said, patting her hand. "You know I am. What do you remember about him? Did he wear a medallion?"

"No. Not that I could remember anyway. I was only five."

"Well, I wouldn't think he was a royal fae. What color was his hair? Blond like yours?"

"No. Dark like yours and Deveron's."

Ritasia frowned. "He couldn't have been from the Denkar."

"I don't think so. He called them—you—barbarians."

"Unless he was one of us and was angered that we might kill you."

"I hadn't thought of that. Would he be related to you then?"

Ritasia smiled. "No, most likely not. There are tons of lines in the Denkar that are not related to us. Just like in the case of humans, too much inbreeding can cause problems. That's why the royals marry into other kingdoms…well, and to make alliances. And I know everyone who is closely related. If a male fae disappeared for five years, I would have known."

"What other kingdoms have dark-haired fae?"

"Oh, all of them. Some more than others."

"That doesn't help."

"No, if he was a royal, that would help." Ritasia fingered her gold medallion.

Alicia considered the diagrams in her father's journal. "Which fae have the symbol of the dragon?"

Ritasia narrowed her eyes. "Why?"

"It's one of the symbols he drew in his journal. He drew yours, Venicia's, and three others. But none were of Neferon. I'm wondering if there's a clue in that."

"Maybe. What did he say about Morcalon?"

"Who?"

"The fae of the dragon."

"Nothing. He just drew the symbol. Maybe he didn't know much about them. Just that they existed."

"Every fae knows of them. They are the most warrior race of all of the fae."

"I thought the dark fae were."

Ritasia smiled. "I guess it depends on who's writing the history."

"Oh." Alicia hadn't considered that, but she supposed Ritasia was right.

Ritasia took a deep breath. "The dragon fae are our sworn enemy. Have been forever."

"Oh."

"What other symbols did he draw?"

"The cobra, hawk, and griffin."

Ritasia stared at the ground, then looked up at Alicia. "All the major kingdoms, but one."

"And Neferon isn't one."

"No."

"Which did he leave out?"

"The sphinx. The fae of the sphinx are said to be of the earliest civilization. As peaceful as the ones of the dragon are warlike. Where the sphinx fae try to keep peace, the dragon fae prefer fighting. Lorelei's father is a sphinx fae. Her mother, of course, is Venician, of the gargoyle fae." Ritasia tapped her fingers on the bench. "Your father wrote about each of the major kingdoms?"

"Except for Morcalon and the sphinx fae."

"Tell me what he said about the others. Maybe that'll give us a clue."

Just then, Deveron and Lorelei returned. She looked miffed as her mouth turned down at the corners. Deveron didn't seem to be any happier.

"I believe we just took a race through the gardens. As far as I'm concerned," Lorelei said, her voice verging on whining as she wiped her flushed face with a lace-edged cloth, "neither of us won."

Alicia smiled. "Then it was a tie. Neither of you will be upset by the results."

Ritasia laughed.

Deveron frowned at his sister. "You may leave now, dear sister. I will take care of our cousin."

"No," Lorelei nearly snapped. When everyone looked at her, she smiled. "Tonight we shall have a grand ball...a masked affair. I insist that Ritasia and your cousin attend. We will all have such fun."

"I will stay," Ritasia said, but her voice was not cheerful. More than this, she sounded concerned and Deveron's face appeared to mirror this.

Evidently, they knew Lorelei was up to something, and Alicia hadn't a clue. She envisioned it was something wicked.

"I don't dance well," Deveron said.

Alicia couldn't imagine the dark fae hunk wouldn't be able to dance. He appeared to be the kind of guy who could do anything with great success. But she wondered why Ritasia didn't jump in to confirm Deveron's claim.

"Nonsense," Lorelei said. "I saw you dance with Princess Nevian last year and believe me, every marriageable young lady watched the two of you. I was green with envy that I could not catch your eye as I was too young."

"How old are you?" Alicia asked, surprised that the girl would have been too young the year previously, but was now being foisted on Deveron.

Lorelei tilted her chin up. "Sixteen. And you?"

Then Alicia noticed the fae didn't have the golden fae ring around her eyes. Why not?

"Seventeen," Alicia said, still trying to discern the meaning of the fae having no ring. She glanced over at the ladies who waited on Lorelei. Both had the shimmering rings encircling their eyes. What did it mean?

Deveron smiled at Alicia's answer.

Did he like that she was more his age? Come to think of it, she didn't know his age.

Loud brass bells rang out across the castle grounds, sending a shock wave through Alicia.

Lorelei pulled Deveron past Alicia and Ritasia toward the castle. "Time to eat."

Ritasia helped Alicia to stand, then looped her arm through hers. "You stick close to me, Alicia, whatever happens."

"Why do you want to help me? I thought I'd made you pretty mad when I called you a jealous fae, then ignored you existed. Of course I only did so because I'd come to my senses and realized I should have held my tongue in the first place."

Ritasia giggled. "I'm like my brother. I don't get mad, I get—"

"Even."

Ritasia's eyes sparkled in amusement. "You must have realized I was pretty shocked to hear you speak to me. I knew I wasn't a jealous fae, for one thing. How could I be jealous over my brother's interest in a human girl? In truth, Deveron's escapades liven up fae life, which can be rather dull at times. Why else would we visit the humans?"

She took a deep breath and looked pleased with herself. "Now you are irking Lorelei more than I ever could. I will help you to widen the rift and protect your back at the same time."

"Great. I already have your mother and all her people ready to do me serious harm. And if she discovers your brother is irritating the fae that your mother intends for your brother to marry all because of me—"

"Yes, well, fae business can be rather dangerous at times. Aren't you game? I suspect you wish to find your father. Deveron and I will help you in that endeavor. And I further believe you have no more desire that Deveron marry the witchy Lorelei than I wish to wed her despicable brother. And finally, I don't think you're the type of human who flinches when faced with danger."

Well it depended on the danger. Snakes and poisonous spiders

Alicia flinched at.

As they walked into the great hall filled with fae courtiers dressed in their evening finery, a red-haired male, who looked very much like Lorelei, approached them. He reminded Alicia of a stick figure she might have drawn with a mop of unruly, curly red hair that rested at his shoulders. Maybe that's why Lorelei kept her hair confined. It was a bushel of red frizz. Okay, so that was catty. It might be very pretty.

Though she hoped it was not.

"Prince Phillinois," Ritasia said, curtseying.

Alicia quickly attempted to copy Ritasia's graceful curtsey, but because her equilibrium was still slightly out of whack, she ended up sitting very quickly in her shimmering purple gowns on the terra cotta tile floor.

Ritasia hurried to help her up. "My dear cousin, Princess Alicia, who is ill," Ritasia introduced her to the prince.

Alicia was sure her face looked feverish and perfectly ill as she unconsciously played her part so well. She caught Deveron's actions as he hurried to help her. His face looked quite aghast. And Lorelei attempted to prevent him from going to Alicia's aid as she dug her claws into his arm.

Prince Phillinois stared at Alicia for a moment, then nodded. He turned his attention to Ritasia and smiled. But it wasn't a warm smile, rather a look like she should be pleased she would be his. "You will sit beside me at the high table."

"And Alicia," Ritasia said, pointedly.

Alicia liked the fae's determination when Ritasia was on her side.

He glanced at Alicia with condescension. "And your cousin."

When they reached the high table clothed in a shimmering gold cloth, the king and queen were absent. Ritasia explained to Alicia they were away on holiday.

But then the shuffling of seats began.

Deveron insisted Alicia sit between him and his sister to ensure they could *both* watch her during the meal—owing to the fact she had collapsed in the great hall already.

Lorelei seemed more than a little perturbed as Alicia assumed the girl wanted to sequester Deveron as far away from her as she could.

When they settled down in their embroidered golden seats, the feast began.

Deveron immediately leaned over Alicia and spoke to Ritasia. "Be sure she only eats part of your food. And she can share mine."

Lorelei would have Alicia poisoned? The viper. But Ritasia had said the fae liked dangerous games. And what if Alicia died at the meal?

Then she thought of her grand entrance to the great hall. Again her cheeks burned just thinking about falling on her butt. Here she thought she'd mastered a pretty good curtsey, until her knees melted into heated butter, and she collapsed in a non-too graceful manner.

Deveron grasped her hand and squeezed. "Do not eat any portion of your meal, nor sip from your goblet."

He wouldn't have to tell her twice.

She nodded.

He leaned over and whispered in her ear, "You are playing your fragile role very well, my faery princess."

She poked him in the ribs and scowled at him. How could he mock her after she had thoroughly embarrassed herself in front of the entire fae court of Venicia?

He chuckled, then handed her his goblet.

Lorelei said, "She has her own."

"Yes, but she prefers to drink from mine."

Lorelei's green eyes narrowed with vengeance. Alicia had no doubt whatsoever that the spiteful fae would speed up Alicia's demise if she could manage it. Alicia also noticed that the steward watched her, too. Had he a hand in this? Most assuredly. Alicia was from a minor royal house, or at least pretending to be. Would it be presumed that no one would miss her horribly if she took a fatal bite from her meal?

Ritasia handed Alicia a wedge of cheese.

Despite the seriousness of the situation, or perhaps because of it,

Alicia couldn't help the fondness she felt for the dark fae sister and brother for attempting to keep her safe. They genuinely seemed to like her. Or was it just another deadly faery game?

Stir up the Venicians as neither Deveron nor Ritasia wished to wed their royal offspring? Use Alicia as the wedge? The human girl of no consequence?

She groaned inwardly with the notion.

"How are you feeling now?" Deveron asked her as he slipped his spoon underneath a stuffed mushroom, then leveled it at her lips.

She reached for the spoon, but he refused to give it to her. Her gaze shifted from the mushroom resting on the spoon to Deveron's face and that roguish grin he so often wore in her presence.

How could she not find the dark fae so totally appealing? She had to face it. She was a genuine human sap when it came to his charms.

"Open up," he said pointing the spoon at her sealed lips.

"I'm not a baby bird."

He chuckled. "Come on, Alicia. Please me."

She folded her arms. Please him? Who did he think he was? Okay, so he was a dark fae prince of one of the major kingdoms. Didn't matter to her. She didn't need to please him unless it was her idea. "You're making me look foolish."

"I am not. A fae who offers sustenance to another is being—"

Ritasia interrupted, "Chivalrous beyond reason."

But the way she spoke, Alicia wondered if Ritasia hadn't a different sentiment in mind. Her brows were raised as if she didn't think her brother was being chivalrous, rather something else.

Alicia wished she knew more about fae culture.

"Go ahead, Alicia. It'll irritate Lorelei all the more," Ritasia whispered in her ear.

All right. That she could do. Particularly since the vamp might be trying to poison her.

Alicia took the mushroom and enjoyed the sautéed breading and cheese-covered shrimp stuffed into the mushroom cap.

He watched her enjoy the morsel, then smiled. "See now? That wasn't so bad was it?"

She noticed then that Lorelei's face had reddened to the same color as the brilliant roses in the garden.

Good. Was that Deveron's plan? To stir up the witch who was trying to poison her? What if she wasn't?

But then again, the dark fae would know better than she would.

Alicia grinned. "Can I have another?"

She couldn't be sure, but she thought she heard Lorelei hiss a curse under her breath.

CHAPTER 9

Deveron felt remorse for what he was putting poor Alicia through. How could a human hope to understand the ways of the fae...the dark, dangerous, deadly ways they handled matters when they so chose to sway a situation in their favor?

He needed her to help ensure he'd never wed Lorelei. Though he hadn't realized how much she'd turn the stakes. Especially since he'd only kept her with him initially to prevent her from being caught by his mother and her royal guard. No telling what the queen would decide to do with Alicia. He was bound and determined to protect her, just like he'd promised. Another dark fae quality—extreme loyalty despite the dangerous consequences.

Alicia was a natural at fae games and couldn't have done a better job if she'd been born of the fae. But if Lorelei injured her, he'd never forgive himself.

When he'd fed Alicia the mushroom, he'd done it in fun—at least that's what he'd told himself. Though he knew what the significance of his actions meant to the fae, he was certain Alicia didn't. At first he was afraid Ritasia would try to stop him. But then she seemed to realize he was pushing the issue forward as forcefully as he could. Never would he consider marrying Lorelei. If he showed Alicia endearments that he would only share with the one he had chosen for his own, then Lorelei would come to realize, she'd lost him.

Of course, if Alicia had known what his action had meant, she might not have gone along with it. But then again when she realized how mad it had made Lorelei, she'd played the game with great enthusiasm…pointing at this food or that on his plate and smiling and laughing with gusto. He'd never enjoyed a female's company so much, either human or fae. The only problem was that her previous state of being so incapacitated seemed to vanish with every bite.

Her clear green eyes shimmered with frivolity and her full pink lips shined with a glossy coating of peach wine—his peach wine. Her tongue swept over her lips absent-mindedly, and he wanted to taste her lips again.

He forced himself to drop that notion before he started a virtual war between his kingdom and the Venicians. It was one thing to take care of his cousin, another to seduce her at the table.

"You seem to be feeling better," he whispered in her ear.

"I am. I'm afraid I've lost some of my fragility, however."

He smiled. "You will have to regain some of it, but I'm glad you are feeling more yourself."

His next major worry was the masked ball though. What had Lorelei intended for that? He was certain he would have to remove Alicia from the deadly fae game sooner than later. Fae had played these games for centuries. The human girl wouldn't stand a chance. But he was still trying to figure out where to take her to ensure her security. One wrong move could mean imprisonment for her or worse.

"You stick close to either Ritasia or me for the entire ball," he whispered to her.

"Do you think someone will try something?"

"I don't know. But always stay alert." Somehow between his sister and him, they would have to maintain Alicia's well-being.

Was he being conceited to think he could keep her safer at his side than if he returned her home? No, he knew it would be only a matter of time before the Denkar learned where Alicia lived. If she'd been alone, he would never be able to save her.

If he'd been as evil as Alicia seemed to think the dark fae kind were, he wouldn't have cared. But his people weren't evil like that. Well, not all of his people. And certainly not his sister and him.

He took a deep breath as he watched Alicia sip some more of his wine.

He couldn't fall for a fae-knower. He wouldn't allow his thoughts to drift in that dangerous direction. Not that anyone would kill him for it. But Alicia would be in more danger than before.

*   *   *

After the meal, Lorelei managed to pull Deveron away for a game of archery, a favorite pastime of the nobility.

"Do you want to shoot, too?" Ritasia asked Alicia as they sauntered to the target practice, following Deveron, Lorelei, and her maids from some distance back.

Alicia shook her head.

"Oh, I should have asked first, do you know how to shoot?"

"Yes."

Ritasia's brows rose in question. "Well?"

"Yes, I'm good at it, but why would I want to?"

Ritasia smiled. "Because if you can shoot better than Lorelei, and she *is* a pretty good shot, it could vex her further."

"Don't you think she hates me enough already?"

"No," both Ritasia and Alicia said at the same time.

They laughed and folded their arms while they watched first Lorelei shoot, then Deveron.

Deveron's muscles flexed so beautifully as he concentrated on the target that Alicia couldn't help but admire his form.

He shot 50 yards farther than Lorelei, which was to be expected being that he was a stronger male.

Lorelei grinned at him, then leaned over and kissed his cheek.

Alicia squelched the urge to slap her. Again, she chided herself for the insane surge of jealousy that erupted deep inside of her. She couldn't, wouldn't allow herself to grow soft where the dark fae was concerned. *He is evil*, she reminded herself. And beautiful.

She sighed deeply. So she could fantasize over him, pretend he was the cutest guy she'd met in a long time, that kissed her with the kind of passion only…only, jeez, only a dark fae could kiss her like.

She'd have to take second best. Only problem was a human might end up coming in a distant tenth place.

Ugh. Stop thinking about him, Alicia. He is not in your league. Not in your realm. He has taken you prisoner on the pretense he must protect you. And he's evil! Maybe in a sweet kind of evil way.

She could protect *herself*, thank you very much.

"I would have you by my side protecting me from my enemy any day, Deveron." Lorelei turned to Alicia and said, "Do you shoot?"

"A little. But you would find me poor competition."

"Ritasia is poor competition," Lorelei said with a malevolent gleam in her eye.

Deveron's jaw tightened.

Alicia ground her teeth, furious that Lorelei would put Ritasia down so. "Then perhaps I would do better to be pitted against Ritasia."

"All right. Since I have already gone once, you go against Ritasia first. If you are better than she, you can go against me."

Alicia shook her head.

"Are you afraid to compete with me?" Lorelei tilted her chin up with the taunt.

Afraid of the viper? No!

Deveron seemed torn between wanting to see Alicia prove herself better than Lorelei, but not wanting to see her fail miserably and lose to the snooty princess.

It didn't matter one way or another to Alicia. She'd do her best, and maybe, she could win. Or not. At least she'd show she wasn't afraid of the competition.

"All right." She'd won several competitions in archery when she was in Girl Scouts, but the fae bows were thinner, more curved and slightly twisted. She wasn't sure if being human would make a difference, and she was afraid never having practiced on a fae bow

64

would give her a decided disadvantage.

Ritasia went first, and as Lorelei had said, she did poorly. Alicia thought if she lived long enough, she might be able to give Ritasia some pointers at some other time.

Alicia patted Ritasia on the arm. "Good job. Maybe I can practice with you later."

Ritasia's face lighted up with impish delight.

Of course if Alicia did poorly…

Lorelei glared at her and folded her arms.

Alicia twisted the bow around in her hands. "I've never used a bow quite like this before."

"Oh? I thought the Neferonians used the same bows as we do."

"I've become quite fond of human bows," Alicia said. "So I'm not sure how well I'll do at this."

"Have you never used a fae bow?" Deveron asked, his voice concerned.

Though she assumed he already knew this. But then maybe he said so to get her off the hook with Lorelei.

"No, I haven't," Alicia said.

"Then take a practice shot first," Deveron said, and she was sure he was trying to rescue her.

Lorelei laughed with dark humor. "Take several. Take a week. We are not doing this for any kind of reward. So be bold."

Alicia aimed the arrow, but the bow twisted in such a strange way, the missile dropped onto the ground only a few feet away.

Muttered chuckles from Venician onlookers resulted.

Her blood heated. She turned to Ritasia, whose wide eyes and parted lips gave Alicia the impression her poor attempt at archery horrified the dark fae princess. Alicia smiled at her, trying to reassure her it didn't matter to the human how poorly she'd done. "Well, Ritasia, let me amend my offer. I can show you how to shoot well with a *human* bow."

Ritasia nodded with only a smidgeon of a smile. Alicia feared Ritasia was still worried about the outcome of the game.

Alicia handed the bow to a servant, done forever with fae archery competitions.

Lorelei said, "No, you are to shoot against me now."

"*If* I won against Ritasia I was to shoot against you. I didn't get close."

Lorelei's lips turned into a vile grin. "Amuse me again then."

"Very well. Anything to please you. Go ahead." *Not.*

Lorelei motioned to the target. "After you, as you are my guest."

She was giving Alicia no chance to rest her arms.

Alicia took her stance again, but this time she considered what she'd done wrong the first time. Maybe if she twisted the bow slightly to her right and tilted it up higher, she could compensate for the problem she had initially.

She'd have to practice for weeks to get the hang of the strange faery bow.

But with all eyes on her—as she noticed several more courtiers had gathered to watch the competition of the royals—she hadn't any choice. Shoot the arrow and hope it fell farther than the last few feet at least.

She closed one eye and released the arrow.

CHAPTER 10

Whispered murmurs filled the crowd as Alicia stared at the distance she'd sent the arrow...two feet farther than Deveron's even. She hated to look at Deveron. Would he be upset with her? She had won several archery competitions. She couldn't help that. And she *had* tried to decline playing the game.

Lorelei stared at her with such contempt Alicia figured she could have turned her to stone. She offered the bow to Lorelei.

Lorelei shook her head. "No, my arms are too weary to shoot again."

Deveron rubbed his chin while he considered where her arrow had struck the farther target.

Ritasia looked mortified.

Well, that hadn't gone well.

"Can we do something else?" Alicia asked, handing the bow to the servant again.

"You will shoot against *me*," Deveron said, reclaiming the bow. He didn't seem at all happy.

Alicia's mouth dropped open as she stared at Deveron. Was he miffed at her for beating him? When she was a mere human? And even worse, a human female who had never used a fae bow? Heaven have mercy. What a crisis to his dark male fae heritage.

"It was a lucky shot," Alicia said. "Probably couldn't do it again in a million years."

Lorelei's mutinous expression hadn't changed. Ritasia still seemed ill at ease.

What? If she bested Deveron again, would they hang her at high noon? Had she done some unforgivable deed?

She supposed she was never to best a male fae at archery. So should she hit short this time to give Deveron the chance to prove his superior male archery ability?

Or should she try her best to beat him again?

He pulled back the string and with everyone quiet as a black void in space, he released the arrow. It smacked the wooden stake target, splitting it in two.

Several clapped and expressed their congratulations.

A servant quickly placed another stake the same distance, but Alicia aimed at one several feet farther out. Competition was competition. She didn't figure she'd have mastered the bow this quickly, but perhaps it was just that she knew so well how to apply her skills in archery and it didn't matter the strange shape of bow.

Or not.

It might have been a fluke.

She stopped breathing as she readied her arrow. Everyone else seemed to stop breathing, too.

The arrow whipped through the air and without a breeze stirring, struck its target, beating Deveron's by five feet.

"Again," he said, his tone harsh.

She wanted to remind him she was frail and their ruse was quickly being eroded away. "I'm tired."

"Again," he commanded. This time his firm voice brooked no argument.

Stubborn dark fae with an easily bruised male ego the size of the state of Alaska.

He fired an arrow that hit a stake ten feet beyond hers.

This time she would not play the game. Her arms were wearied, and she would not be commanded by any fae, dark, male, royal, or otherwise, what to do.

Damn his male ego.

She meant to shoot at a much closer target. That's what she meant to do. But somehow her own stubbornness took control of her and made her do it. She aimed, pulled, and struck his arrow, splitting it in two.

Then she handed the bow to the servant and said, "*Next* game?"

Everyone was speechless. No one dared to congratulate the female fae, well human, but they didn't know that. All they knew was she was creating a wedge between their princess and Prince Deveron, so no one would congratulate her. She suspected Deveron was mad at her. Ritasia seemed unduly concerned.

Maybe because Deveron was mad at her.

"It's time for us to retire to our bedchambers and get ready for the ball," Lorelei said.

"I'll share the guestroom with my cousin," Ritasia announced.

Alicia wouldn't look at Deveron. He was a spoiled rotten dark fae who couldn't concede she was a pretty damned good marksman.

Too bad.

"You seem to have regained your strength back quite well," Lorelei said as she grasped Deveron's arm and spoke to Alicia.

"It comes and goes," Ritasia quickly said.

"Does Alicia have a change of gowns? Everyone will know her at the ball if she does not."

Ritasia said, "I have brought a week's worth to Venicia. I'm sure she will find one that appeals."

"No one is to know who anyone else is," Lorelei reminded her.

"I will know her, as I need to watch out for her."

Lorelei nodded.

Ritasia took hold of Alicia's hand and transported her to the bedchambers. The effect wasn't hardly dizzying at all, considering the short distance.

"Are you all right?" Ritasia asked her.

"Yes. I guess we were so close by, it didn't bother me as much."

Ritasia pulled a chest open, then sifted through several gowns.

Alicia watched her, then said, "I guess no one liked it that I beat Deveron in archery. I assumed he didn't either."

"Other things were on his mind."

Alicia studied her as she pulled out a sea green dress.

"To go with your green eyes and blond hair. It should be very fetching." Ritasia handed it to her, then returned to the chest.

Alicia ran her fingers over the silky sheers that covered the satin gown underneath. "What other things were on his mind?"

Ritasia dug around in the chest some more, then pulled out a peach-colored gown. "Like who you are."

Taking a deep breath, Alicia said, "Well, that I would like to know as well."

Ritasia stood. "I think it best if we return you home."

Gone was the fae friendship, just like that? One archery competition, no cheating, and she was no longer wanted by the dark fae? Had they lost interest in the human who could best them at a game? And why even bring her here if they were truly concerned about her safety? Was it all just pretend?

"I would be happy to oblige. Take me there now. Or return me to South Padre Island."

"Deveron would have to approve."

"Why? He doesn't own me."

"In a way, he does."

Alicia squelched the urge to scream and handed the gown back to Ritasia. "Take me home now, please."

"I can't and I won't."

Alicia tapped her foot on the floor. There was nothing worse than being stranded in a place she had no way to get out of. And in no way did she belong to Deveron.

"You and Deveron are mad I did so well at the competition. Why? Was it because I bruised his male ego?"

"It is more than that."

"What?"

Ritasia began to pull off her emerald green gown.

"What?"

"I can't say," Ritasia said with exasperation. "I need to speak with Deveron first."

"I can't return to South Padre or my home without your help, can I?" Or her father's. But she had no way of knowing who he was or where he lived.

Alicia studied the fae who ignored her. "Fine." She headed for the door.

"Wait!" Ritasia's voice was desperate. She was half undressed and couldn't very well chase after Alicia. But Alicia wasn't staying if Ritasia wouldn't confide in her.

"Well?"

"We'll talk with…I'll speak with my brother after the ball."

"Right."

Alicia yanked the door open and headed out of the room.

"Alicia! Wait."

She closed the door behind her. *She* would have a word with Deveron. Why did Ritasia have to act as her intermediary? Was Deveron that mad at Alicia?

CHAPTER 11

Frustrated over having no control over her destiny, Alicia had every intention of seeing Deveron and forcing him to return her home at once. She would make her mother tell her who her father was like she should have done years ago.

She stormed down the hallway, wondering where Deveron could be staying. Then she saw the steward. His gray eyes caught sight of her immediately and widened, though he'd been talking to a guard.

Her skin crawled and an uncontrollable panic filled her with dread. She slowed her pace.

He headed for her with the guard at his side.

She stiffened her resolve. She would ask him where Deveron was located. Easy enough. And then the steward would answer her question in a very civil tongue. Right. There wouldn't be any way he'd want her to visit Deveron at his guest bedchambers, not when he wanted Princess Lorelei to wed the prince.

"Alicia!" Deveron called from some distance behind her.

Relief to hear his voice washed over her like a warm South Padre Island wave, even though his voice was couched in worry.

Had he changed his mind about being angry with her over the archery competition? Didn't matter. She was going home.

She headed in his direction, but he reached her first. Before she could utter a word, he dragged her back to her guest quarters. She tried to break free.

He tightened his grip.

"Let go of me!"

"You are never to be out of Ritasia's or my sight, Alicia. I told you that already."

"I'm sorry you can't deal with my winning at the competition. Well, tying at the last of it anyway," she said haughtily.

"You have no idea the trouble you've stirred up."

"What?" Was this what Ritasia alluded to but wouldn't speak of? What was the matter now?

They arrived back at the chambers, and he opened the door as Alicia squeaked, "Ritasia is changing!"

But Ritasia had already changed into her peach gown and was shoving her sandals on her feet.

"Thank goodness you caught her," Ritasia said.

"Take me home," Alicia said as he pulled her into the room and shut the door. She jerked her arm free.

"We need to discuss this, Deveron," Ritasia said.

"I don't know where else I can take her where she'll be safe." He ran his fingers through his hair.

"What is the matter?" Alicia nearly shouted.

Deveron considered her, then shook his head. "You are a dragon fae. Our greatest enemy."

"Bull. How could I be?"

"Half, I should say. It's the only explanation. Only the female dragon fae can shoot like you can with the bow. No one who had never used a fae bow like that could do what you did. And no female fae could shoot as far and well as you, unless you were a dragon fae. It's an inherited trait."

Alicia sat down hard on a blue velvet chair. A dragon fae. Her father was a dragon fae?

"What if her father is someone of consequence, Deveron? What if he learns his sworn enemy has taken her hostage?"

"Mother will attempt to do the same thing. There could be war," Deveron said.

"Why? My father abandoned me when I was five. He would never know I was with the Denkar as their prisoner or otherwise."

"Spies are prevalent in a castle. Always. I'd bet a year's worth of gold one is on his way to Morcalon right now with news of the female fae pretending to be a Neferon princess. Not only that, but the crown prince and princess of the royal family of Denkar guard her closely. Rumors probably already abound about your strange malady. Are we drugging you? Then as the time wears on you are your perky self again?"

"Then return me home."

Deveron paced across the floor.

"Return me home!"

"No."

"Deveron—"

"No." He turned to Ritasia. "Can you ensure she stays here and changes her gowns?"

She nodded, but wrung her hands.

"Stay! We will take you from here during the height of the ball. Do not, whatever you do, stray from Ritasia."

He stalked out of the room and slammed the door behind him.

She was not a dog. She would not be commanded to stay like a dog!

"You must get changed," Ritasia said, in a much gentler voice.

Alicia folded her arms.

Ritasia's voice changed. "I should have known you were a dragon fae. They're notoriously stubborn."

"Written from their history or yours?"

Ritasia managed a small smile. "If we are to leave here safely," she tried again, "you must do as Deveron says."

"Where are we going after that?"

Ritasia shook her head. "Deveron is the one who gets himself into complicated messes like these, though come to think of it, this is the worse one ever. And usually he figures a way to get himself out again. I'm sure he already has a plan."

* * *

Deveron changed into a black tunic, black trousers, boots and a black wig. After tying his wig hair into a ponytail, he donned a black mask. Then he vanished and reappeared at the entrance to the grand ballroom. One good thing about fae travel, no one would have seen him leave his room while he was wearing his costume.

When he strode into the room, he found it crowded with exuberant masked courtiers eager to guess everyone's identity. He cursed himself for not asking Ritasia what Alicia was wearing to the ball.

At least he'd paid enough attention to know Ritasia wore her favorite peach gown. The unusual color looked well on her. Very rarely did he ever see anyone wearing that shade but her. He assumed he'd find her easily. And where she stood, he'd find Alicia.

Because of the crowd, a good twenty minutes passed before he spied Ritasia. He vanished and reappeared next to her. "Ritasia," he said taking hold of her hand.

The lady giggled and he released her hand at once. "If you wish to me to be the princess, my lord, I would be glad to take her place."

His skin chilled. Where the hell was Ritasia? She wouldn't have changed again unless...

Maybe she was fighting with Alicia to get her to change clothes. He took a deep breath and hurried out of the ballroom with a quick stride toward Alicia's door.

CHAPTER 12

Alicia feared for her life more than ever, knowing that she was half dragon fae. Others, including the Denkar, hated her....or her kind.

Which would mean they hated *her*.

And all because she had wanted to protect her friend, Cassie, from the attentions of a gorgeous, drop dead, dark fae at the beach on their vacation. Next time, she'd let well enough alone.

If there was a next time.

She slipped into the sea green gown, hoping that no one but Deveron and Ritasia would know who she was. "Thank you for letting me borrow another of your gowns, Ritasia, especially knowing what you do about me."

"I have to admit, Alicia, you are not at all like I would imagine the dragon fae would be. Maybe it's because you were not raised by them. Or perhaps even my perception of them is incorrect. All I know is I truly care what happens to you. And so does Deveron."

"He has an odd way of showing it." Alicia smoothed down the wispy sheers that floated into place with seeming reluctance.

Ritasia clipped Alicia's blond hair back with diamond studded hair fasteners. "I'm sure the shock of which fae kingdom you originated from upset him some. I'm not certain either of us would have ever suspected you were a dragon fae." She returned to the chest and shook her head as she pulled two feathered masks from it. "We would never have suggested you take part in archery had we known. Though, I suspect if you came from one of the close lines of Denkar fae, he would be as ruffled." She waved the masks at her. "Either of these? I have others."

"The silver would be fine." She considered Ritasia's words further. "Why would it bother him if I were one of your close relations?"

Ritasia smiled a strange little smile, then handed her the silver mask. "Perhaps Deveron could explain better." She attached a golden mask to her own face.

"I thought you hated me because I was a dragon fae."

"No. Only we're concerned, and rightly so, that the dragon fae will take revenge because we have taken you—with us—for your own well-being, of course. Only they would not see it that way. Are you ready to go?"

Alicia took a deep breath, trying to massage her raw nerves.

"Whatever happens, stay with me at all times."

Alicia had every intention of doing what the dark fae wanted her to do. Despite seeming upset that she was a dragon fae, both Ritasia and her brother appeared to genuinely want to help her. Besides, what choice did Alicia have but to trust them?

Ritasia took her hand, but there was no smile on her lips. Alicia imagined the ball was going to be like entering the lair of the dragon fae for the Denkar kind. Only it was Alicia who had to worry about the Venician fae's intentions.

One wrong move…and Alicia was history.

* * *

Deveron arrived at Alicia's door. Rather than barging in this time, he knocked, not wanting to catch Alicia half-dressed and have her bite his head off in reaction.

When there was no answer, he shoved the door open. The women were gone. Panic spread through him like a twister tore across a Texas plain in the stormy spring.

He returned at once to the ball.

"Are you Joslo?" a lady asked as she grabbed his arm and smiled broadly.

77

"No, my lady." He pulled away.

Then to his further alarm, he saw Micala, not in costume, of course. A guard was trying to remove him from the ballroom for not wearing a mask.

Deveron appeared next to Micala, then hurried him outside of the ballroom. "What's wrong? Where's Cassie?"

"Can we go to the privacy of your guest chambers, my lord?"

Had the royal guard come after Micala, looking for more answers about Alicia? Deveron took his arm and they appeared inside his guest quarters.

"Cassie is back at her home, my lord. But that is not the problem."

"What?"

"Alicia's mother came searching for her. Apparently, she was supposed to spend a couple of days with the girls, but she came early. Here I am entertaining Cassie instead, and there's no sign of Alicia."

"Then what?" Deveron's heart raced as it was, worrying about the women. But if Alicia knew her mother was concerned about her whereabouts…

Yet, Micala would have used his fae magic to make Alicia's mother forget about her. The look on Micala's face indicated it wasn't the worst of their problems.

"She was like a mother grizzly. I've never seen a woman so irate. But that's not all of it, my lord. She's the fae."

"What? I thought it was Alicia's father."

"Apparently not. The woman wore contact lenses to hide her eyes, but she grew so angry, not even the contacts could disguise the fae fire encircling them."

"Does she know which fae you serve?"

"No, my lord. She seemed too shook up. She took Cassie with her, I assume home, and then I came straight here. I think she believed I was just interested in the human girl. We were sharing an ice cream sundae when Alicia's mother found us. I told her I'd never seen Alicia, only Cassie, and befriended her, as I often did when I was bored with fae life.

"She grilled me some more, but I stuck to my story, that I'd found Cassie alone, and made friends with her. I felt sorry for her that she was by herself. I think Alicia's mother believed that perhaps another fae had stolen Alicia away due to her abilities, and made Cassie forget all about her. Anyway, the mother didn't seem to think I had anything to do with Alicia's disappearance."

Deveron paced. "Alicia's a *dragon* fae."

"What?"

"The mother wasn't a royal was she?"

"I saw no medallion, but if she disguised her eyes, I would think she'd hide any other evidence she was a fae. The only thing that's in our favor is she must have broken away from her people. They wouldn't get involved, don't you agree?"

"No. We can't be certain of that." Deveron pointed at a wooden chest. "Find another mask. We've got to locate Alicia and Ritasia in the ballroom and move them at once."

"Where to, my prince?"

Deveron snorted. "Anywhere that we can think of that might be safe."

* * *

As soon as Alicia and Ritasia arrived at the grand ballroom, she feared the worse. The place was crowded. Everyone wore disguises. The sweet waters the women wore scented the air like the faery garden, and faery tunes played, giving the deadly environment a sugar sweet coating. But Alicia knew somewhere in this crowd, Lorelei was waiting to strike at her...like a rattler poised.

Couples danced in the center of the floor, the ladies' gowns rustling with the fae movements, smooth as ballerinas dancing with their gents in a faery all-star cast.

Ritasia nearly cut off the circulation in Alicia's hand she gripped it so tightly. She whispered to Alicia, "Deveron will wear black. As in the bad fae, like your Westerns always depict the unscrupulous cowboy. Bad to the bone in black."

Alicia couldn't help but smile at the thought. He *was* bad. His kisses were so divinely good they were sinfully bad…good, whatever.

And whatever brought that to mind, she had no idea.

But what she wouldn't have given to have his arm wrapped around her waist, keeping her safe right now. Though she appreciated Ritasia's "protection," Alicia was certain her fingers would drop off within a matter of minutes from lack of circulation.

"I don't see anyone wearing black tonight. The fae here appear to like the lighter colors," Alicia said, straining to see the taller males.

"That's precisely why he would wear it. Besides he's trying to keep his dark fae image with you."

Alicia stared at Ritasia. "I don't understand."

Ritasia's lips turned up. "I believe he thinks you are intrigued by the notion he is an evil dark fae. He isn't evil, you know. Any more than I am. Some are, of course, just like some humans are. But, for whatever reason, he is trying to please you. You didn't hear that from me, however."

Twice now Ritasia had alluded to this idea that Deveron cared for Alicia. But how could he, being that she was only half fae, and a dragon fae at that?

Still, her heart beat faster as she considered the possibilities. She and a dark fae? Nah. He was a prince of the dark fae. No way could he see her as anything more than an intriguing mission, an interesting dangerous diversion. Even if he did have…feelings for her, she was certain his queenly mother wouldn't permit him to do anything about it. And what about Alicia's mother? She'd have a fit to think Alicia had fallen…well, she hadn't fallen, maybe was developing a slight crush, a big crush on the dark fae, when Alicia's own fae dad had left her mother so many years ago.

She and Ritasia moved through the standing crowds, trying to see some sign of Deveron. Once Alicia pointed at a man, but Ritasia shook her head. "His clothes are very similar to Deveron's. A nearly black navy blue."

Then Alicia thought she spied Micala. But how could it be

Micala? He was supposed to be at South Padre Island with Cassie.

Just as soon as she saw the man who looked like Micala, another man pulled her away from Ritasia.

"Dance with me," he said, and swung her away on the floor, swirling her to the unfamiliar steps. Her feet barely touched the floor as he glided away from Ritasia.

She only glimpsed the dark fae female briefly, dancing nearby with a man with a blond-haired wig, but a few strands of red hair poked between the blond strands. Prince Phillinois?

If she kept her eyes on Ritasia, and Ritasia watched out for her, maybe they'd be all right.

The blond she danced with held her so tight, she didn't think she would be capable of freeing herself from his grasp. Though she wanted to look for Deveron, too, she figured she'd better keep her eye on Ritasia as Alicia at least knew where she was.

Suddenly the low lights in the ballroom went out, and cries of surprise, then laughter filled the air.

The man who held her, whispered in her ear, "Dragon fae." And then he took her away, somewhere far away as the darkness swirled around her, and she grew dizzy.

Dragon fae echoed in her mind. *Dragon fae…the dark fae may be evil but the dragon fae even more so.*

Die, dragon fae spy…die.

Was she dreaming? Or did the fae speak the words to her, taunting her as he carried her away?

Ritasia. Would Ritasia or Deveron ever know what had become of her? Would they give up the game of protecting the half human/half dragon fae now? Or would they search for her with all of their hearts to free her from the clutches of this man who she knew was truly evil?

She could imagine Ritasia having a fit when she'd lost Alicia as soon as the lights went out. And Deveron, where was he?

She came to the realization that while she was in the faery world she would have to learn to be a faery, just as when she was in the human world, she lived as a human. But how could she live as a faery when she'd never been one before?

It was high time she learned how.

First, if she could get a bow and arrow, she'd shoot the fae who took her away from her friends. She frowned at herself. Is that what being a dragon fae was all about? Warrior-like and vengeful?

Didn't matter. If it saved her butt, she was all for it. "Where can I get a bow and arrow?" she asked.

Her words echoed back to her.

She realized then she was in a dark room, lying shackled to a plank of wood covered in a thin blanket. No longer was she traveling with the fae in the black void. Where was she? And how long had she been here?

But most importantly, how would she get herself out of this place?

CHAPTER 13

Deveron and Micala had found themselves in pitch blackness once they'd returned to the ballroom. Then when the lights turned on again, he knew deep in his heart, they'd lost Alicia.

When he discovered Ritasia dancing with none other than Prince Phillinois, Deveron did the unthinkable and broke in on the dance.

"I have an urgent matter to discuss with my sister," Deveron said.

"For Rastonion's sake, Deveron. Do you mind? Talk to her after we finish the dance," the Venician prince retorted.

Ritasia pulled free. "I will return."

Deveron quickly wrapped his arm around her waist, and grabbed Micala's arm, then transported them to his guest chambers. He released both at once.

They pulled off their masks and deposited them in his chest.

"I don't think there's any mistaking what has happened," Deveron said, trying not to sound as bitter as he felt. How could a half human, half dragon fae stir him up so? He had promised to protect her. That was the only reason, he assured himself. And a dark fae always kept his promise.

"I was sure I heard her cry out," Ritasia said. Her eyes grew tearful. "Phillinois wouldn't release me to go to her, and the man who'd taken her from my grasp, I thought was one of the palace guards. It was hard to tell from his mask."

"Did you see his faery dust trail?"

"Yes, silver with a touch of auburn."

"Can you pick up the trail?"

She nodded. "I couldn't get free from Phillinois. He knew I was trying to go to Alicia's aid, and he had no intention of letting me do so."

"Let's go then before the trail grows cold. We have twenty-four hours to find her before we lose the trail completely."

If he had anything to say about it, they would find Alicia within the hour. Being a human wouldn't equip her for the hostile way a fae could treat her. Would her instincts of being a dragon fae begin to surface? She would need them to survive, he feared.

"Ready?" He slipped his arm around Ritasia's waist, then grabbed hold of Micala's arm. They both nodded and together they transported to the ballroom, appearing only briefly to find the beginning of the faery dust trail left by the fae who'd taken Alicia hostage.

The music had stopped and everyone stood speaking to one another, but as soon as the dark fae royals were noticed, even the conversation ceased.

"We shall return," Deveron said to Phillinois, then vanished again with his sister and Micala.

They stopped numerous times at the places that the man who had taken Alicia had rested. As they stood on a parapet of the Neferon castle overlooking the Obian Sea, Deveron finally remarked, "It appears he worried we might follow him. I only hope that someone else hasn't taken Alicia from him to confuse us."

Ritasia shook her head and pointed at the trail. "There is still only one. He seems to be traveling alone with her. We appear to be only about an hour behind him, as bright as his trail is."

Deveron took a deep breath. "Let's continue, shall we?"

A dark-haired woman ran across the wall walk headed straight for Deveron, smiling broadly.

"Lady Minxsta," he said under his breath. He definitely didn't want their busybody distant cousin to sidetrack them.

"Prince Deveron, Princess Ritasia," she said, grinning from ear to ear and curtseyed deeply at the same time. "Whatever are you doing here? You must come and see—"

"We are on a most urgent mission, Lady Minxsta," Deveron said, curtly.

"You wouldn't happen to have seen a guard from the royal palace of Venicia arrive here with a blond-haired female wearing sea green gowns, would you have?" Ritasia asked, politely.

"Why yes. Do tell, what is going on? Before one of our guards could question the man, as the young girl seemed extremely unwell, the man and she vanished. Do not tell me that he had taken her against her will, and you are attempting to rescue the poor girl?"

Before any could answer her, she looked from one royal to the other, then smiled. "Ooooh, how intriguing. Is she a princess from another kingdom? Why would you wish to be the ones to rescue her? Is she—"

"We must go before the trail grows cold," Deveron said, abruptly.

The woman tugged at a dark curl draped over her shoulder, then smiled again. "He wore a silver tunic and butternut breeches. His hair was blond, but streaked with a few strands of gray. And he had a strange, small, upturned nose. Looked way too small for a man-sized face. I guess you know what the young lady looks like."

"Lady Minxsta, we really must be—"

"The girl, who is she? She looked terribly unwell."

He knew they had to depart or be caught up in a conversation with the lady for hours. And yet he couldn't leave until he heard more about Alicia's condition. "Yes?"

This seemed to spur the lady on to new delights of storytelling. The fact that her favorite prince and princess cousins would be interested in what she had to say…

She would talk about it for days at court.

"Oh, yes, well, the poor little thing looked terribly frazzled. He held her tightly against his chest as she looked as limp as a starved ear of corn. But even at that, she struggled to free herself from him, and I, well and one of our guards, were concerned she was being held against her will. And now with your appearance, we learn she was. Oh the poor little thing. She squeaked out something about needing a bow and arrow...I think. It was awfully hard to understand her. And of course, that didn't make much sense."

Deveron glanced at Ritasia who took a deep breath.

"Anything else?"

"Only one thing. I thought it was an awfully odd thing to do. No one does such a thing when we are among our own kind. Never. It was just so queer."

"What?" Deveron tried to keep his tone of voice reasonable, but the lady was pushing him to the brink.

Ritasia ran her hand over his arm to try to calm him. He didn't need calming. He needed to know what was so odd!

"She turned invisible. Now, don't you think that strange? I mean, here she is as visible as you or me, but then her fae aura surrounds her, clearly indicating she's turned invisible to the human eye. Of course, I attributed it to the man's taking her hostage and wearing her out with his transporting her, possibly even having drugged her. She did look in pretty sad shape. So maybe her senses were out of balance."

He glanced at Ritasia whose eyes couldn't have grown any bigger. "Ritasia, we must go."

She opened her mouth to speak, then nodded.

"Lady Minxsta, as always a pleasure," Deveron said.

She smiled broadly and curtseyed low. "Please come back soon with the poor little thing. We will make her most welcome. Oh, do you need some of the royal guard to go with you? You really shouldn't be the ones traipsing across faery kingdoms, trying to bring her home. Where is her home, anyway?"

Deveron made a curt bow to the lady, not wishing to get drawn into an all-day discussion, then transported Ritasia and Micala once again.

When they stopped in a garden of another fae minor kingdom, Ritasia said, "What does it mean, Deveron? Why would she now be invisible?"

"She is seventeen. Remember when we were first that age? That's when we began to gain some of our powers. We are many years older now, but she really *is* seventeen. I appear eighteen and have been that for years. You are nineteen...the same thing. But she is the real magical seventeen."

"Are you saying she's to be immortal like us?"

"No, only that being half fae, it seems her abilities are just now appearing."

"So she can transport herself?"

He shook his head. "I don't know." He pointed at the ground. "Here's the guard's trail. We see no faery dust for Alicia. She doesn't leave a trail. Maybe being only half fae, she never will. She may never be able to transport herself like we can either. And even if she's able, it may be months before she can."

Micala stretched his arms. "He seems to be criss-crossing the continent. Do you think he'll settle down soon?"

"I hope so," Deveron said, looking at where the trail led south. "But I'm sure when we find Alicia, he'll be long gone or fear our wrath should we locate her."

"I hope they've fed her," Ritasia said, her voice ragged with weariness. "They won't know she's half human and needs to eat. It's a good thing we can eat to enjoy the food, or leave it alone. But I don't imagine she can live without it entirely."

Deveron frowned. He hadn't considered how fragile her human half could make her. "Then we mustn't lose any more time in locating her."

CHAPTER 14

"What have we here," a rough-sounding man said in the dark as Alicia tried to wake. Disoriented, she had no idea where she was. She lay on something hard. When she tried to rise, chains attached to cold metal bracelets that wrapped around her wrists prevented her from moving too far.

She came to the sinking realization she was most likely in a dungeon as the smell of damp earth and decaying matter assaulted her.

The man struck a match, then lighted a lantern. A bulldog-looking man with dark brown hair and cold gray eyes stared at her.

Was he a dark fae?

He wore no medallion. But then he wouldn't. Not if he was just a guard or something.

She glanced down at her clothes. Gone were Ritasia's beautiful sea green gowns, her hair clips and the golden medallion emblem of the Neferon minor royalty. Now Alicia wore a dingy brown wool tunic and brown trousers and a pair of moccasin-like leather shoes.

Alicia's stomach revolted as the bile rose to her throat when she breathed in some more of the nauseously putrid odor. Her throat was parched, and she wondered how long she'd been in this prison.

"Dragon fae," the man sneered.

"Where am I?"

He motioned to the door. Another man, this one tall and thin, escorted a woman into the room. Her ash blond hair was woven into a single braid that trailed down her back. Her eyes were nearly the same olive green as Alicia's and widened to see her as a splinter of recognition flitted across them. Did the woman recognize her? As in, she looked familiar like a relative of someone the woman already knew?

Alicia's skin crawled with the idea that she might be known by a race of fae she'd never met.

The woman wore clothes similar to Alicia—fae prison garb? She appeared to be not much older than Alicia. And she was a prisoner, too, as her hands were manacled. The woman took a deep breath and bowed her head slightly in greeting.

Alicia had only seen males do that when they greeted royalty or lords that outranked them. She was certainly not royalty. And if she had been, the woman should have curtseyed to her. Was the woman trying to signal her in some way? Her eyes remained riveted to Alicia as if she was trying to determine who she was, or where she had seen her before.

"Do you know this dragon fae?" the bulldog of a man asked, his voice irritatingly gruff.

"She is not one of my people," the woman said, with firm confidence.

And yet Alicia sensed the woman meant just the opposite. She could have sworn the woman recognized her.

"She has the archery skills of one of your kind," the man argued.

"That may be so, but I have never seen the woman before in my life." She stepped closer to Alicia. "Let me see your hand."

Alicia showed her the palm of her hand, wondering what that had to do with anything. The woman squeezed her hand, then whispered, "Make a fist."

Alicia did as the woman commanded. As soon as she did, she felt a thin metal object in her hand. A key? Was the dragon fae trying to help her to escape?

Why wouldn't the dragon fae escape herself using the key? Why aid a total stranger?

Because, though the woman said she didn't know her, she

assumed the woman thought otherwise. And Alicia had found the fae were inordinately curious creatures.

"I don't know her," the woman said, matter-of-factly. "She might have been at one of the minor kingdoms. She is not from the royal kingdom of Morcalon."

"Put this one back in her cell," the guard said.

The woman tilted her chin up with a proud air, then cast a nearly imperceptible smile at Alicia.

The other guard roughly escorted the woman out of the cell, and Alicia felt for her, wanting to protect her at the same time.

"Where am I?" Alicia asked, turning her attention to the bulldog guard.

"The dungeon where all good dragon fae belong."

"The dungeon at Venicia?"

"It would have been the first place Prince Deveron would have looked. No, you are far from there. But you will not interfere with Princess Lorelei's plans to wed the dark fae prince any further."

"What will become of me?" She shouldn't have asked. She imagined the guard wouldn't really be privy to court justice. On the other hand, she couldn't help but want to know how bad things could get.

He smiled a despicably sinister smile. "You wouldn't want to know."

Yeah, she did…well, kind of. She had to know how desperate she should be.

But she also wanted him to remove his ugly carcass out of the cell and leave her alone so she could unclench her fist and see if the dragon fae did indeed press a key into her hand.

"Sleep well, false princess. Word will be sent at once to Queen Irenis. I'm certain she will want to know more about you and your relationship with her son, spy. Rest assured, she won't be as nice as me."

He walked out of the room and slammed the door shut.

A warm sunlight began to glow faintly in the distance through a large low window. Why would they have windows with no bars?

Because the fae who were prisoners were manacled and had no chance at escape. Besides, if a prisoner did manage to free his or herself, she wouldn't need a window. The prisoner would just transport herself. If they were a whole fae, unlike her.

She shivered. The chill in the air cloaked her in a frigid blanket. As soon as he left, she opened her hand and smiled to see a small key. She twisted it in the lock on her left manacle and heard a click as it unlocked it, felt a smidgeon of relief—she was far from being free— then she quickly worked on the other.

But if the door were locked and guarded, she'd only have the window as a means of escape. Hopefully she didn't reside in a tower with sheer sides, no way to climb down, and a hundred foot or more drop to a rocky death.

She threw the manacles aside and hurried to the window.

She was no longer dizzy, though her stomach growled, and she felt she'd swallowed tons of cotton, her mouth was so dry.

Peering out the window, she found a narrow ledge that skirted the building. Good thing she wasn't afraid of heights. She looked down. The cliff had plenty of crags for handholds and footholds. It appeared easy enough to climb down the sixty feet or so to the base of the cliff where forest ringed the tower.

When she leaned her head farther out, she could make out another window. Another cell? Maybe the one where the dragon fae resided? She had to return the key to her and help her escape also.

Alicia was glad now for the clothes she wore. It would enable her to climb down the mountain so much more easily than if she was wearing Ritasia's gowns.

Her heart sank as she thought about Ritasia and Deveron. Even if she escaped the prison, then what? She had no idea where she was, or where she could go. And without her father's help, she couldn't even return to her human world.

She climbed through the stone window and clung to the cool, rough stone face as she made her way along the narrow ledge to the next window.

The sun lightened the sky further as the cool breeze began to warm.

She could do this. When she reached the window, she listened first, to ensure no guard was in the room. Not hearing any sound, she peeked in.

In the cell, just as stark as Alicia's, the dragon fae female reclined on a hard wooden plank. Her gaze shifted from the ceiling to Alicia as soon as she began to climb in through the window.

"Why do you come for me?" The fae hurried off the bed. "Escape!"

Alicia strode across the floor, her heart hammering with worry they might get caught. "How could I do that when you so generously aided me in escaping?" She shoved the key into the fae's manacle.

"What is your name?" the fae asked.

"Alicia." She opened the first of the manacles, then worked on the other.

"Alicia," the fae murmured. "Princess Alicia." She curtsied.

The woman had mistaken her for a princess.

"I'm Countess Salimina, at your service."

"I'm afraid you've mistaken me for someone else."

"There is no mistake." The countess glanced down at the floor, then took a steadying breath. She shifted her attention back to Alicia. "Meet me at the gates of Crislis Castle. I'll escort you inside. The kingdom of Morcalon awaits you, though I do not know the reception you will get there. Still, they've been forewarned and will be expecting you."

Forewarned? About her? Now what?

The countess gave another royal courtesy, then disappeared.

"Wait!" Alicia circled the floor. "I can't travel like that." She hadn't expected the fae to vanish so quickly. But would the countess have aided Alicia's escape had she known Alicia was only half fae? Or was that what the fae meant about not knowing how the dragon fae kind would receive her? Would they wish to destroy her like Queen Irenis undoubtedly would?

Voices near the cell drew Alicia's attention. Men's voices. The bulldog fae's gruff voice.

She bolted for the window.

CHAPTER 15

Alicia had no idea what the forests of the fae kingdom here would be filled with, but it couldn't be as bad as the dungeon she attempted to flee.

When she dangled a leg over the windowsill, a key jangled in the lock of the metal door to the cell. She nearly fell off the ledge when she jumped through the window. Would they find her here?

She began the arduous climb down the steep cliff face.

"The dragon fae's escaped! Check the other one's cell!" the bulldog fae shouted.

She realized then, no one would expect her to climb out the window. She would have transported herself like the other fae did. At least that's what the guard would assume.

A door slammed against the wall in her former cell.

"She's gone from here!" a man shouted.

Curses followed.

"Get a dark fae tracker! They're the only ones who can track a faery dust trail."

They'd never find her. She smiled. No fae dust. But then her smile faded. What about the countess? Would they catch her?

She gripped the ledge as she stretched her foot lower to reach another rock jutting out—a perfect foothold.

She'd inched down eight feet maybe when a man shouted, "The dragon fae, who was being held for Queen Irenis, left no trail."

"What?" the bulldog fae shouted. "That's impossible."

"Yes, it is. Quite impossible. And yet somehow she's managed it. The other I can follow."

"I want the one Queen Irenis is sending an escort for. She'll have all of our hides over this."

The other man said, "I can do nothing about the one. There is not a speck of fae dust to follow."

"Find the other. Maybe where she's gone, the other has followed."

"At once."

Alicia hoped the dark fae wouldn't locate the countess. She assumed no one would find the half human who couldn't leave a faery dust trail.

But she was dead wrong.

Though plenty of foot and handholds aided her long, tedious journey, her arms wearied from the climb. She guessed she'd already climbed for a good half hour when she thought she heard a horse's soft whicker.

Horses meant riders. And riders meant humans. Or so she assumed. Faeries didn't ride horses, did they?

But what if they did? What if they were the fae who owned the dungeon? She glance up to survey the tower. Stone walls rose on either side of the tower enclosing a fortress. She could see three more towers. Which fae owned this castle? Were they from a minor or one of the major kingdoms?

The horse whinnied again. She shouldn't look down. What if dozens of fae soldiers waited for her to fall to her death, or if she made it to the bottom of the cliff, arrest her?

What choice did she have? Return to the dungeon tower window and be clapped again in irons? Or could she find her way around the ledge skirting the castle walls? Then what?

Whoever stood below her watched every move she made. Though she was surprised no one seemed to alert the guard in the dungeon.

Were they humans then?

She couldn't help herself. She looked down.

Men and women dressed in typical fae garments—tunics and breeches for the men, sheer, silky gowns for the women, identified them as fae. At least thirty rode horses, six of whom were women.

A hunting party? Several had bows and arrows.

Did she serve as the most interesting prey for the morning's catch?

Several of the fae who observed her antics laughed. *Okay.* So they were undoubtedly courtiers of the castle—owing to the fancy fabrics used in making their clothes.

And she was their morning entertainment. No wonder no one alerted the guard. Whoever heard of a fae making an escape attempt like a human would?

That notion sent a shard of ice into her heart. If they realized she was only a half-fae, whoever was in charge might give the order to terminate her.

She hesitated, undecided as to what to do next. But the longer she held on to her precarious holds, the more tired she became. Still, she had no intention of climbing down all that way, just to be taken prisoner again.

Alicia reached to her right instead of down.

Everyone was completely silent below her.

A rock pulled loose and skittered down to the base of the cliff.

A woman gasped.

Then silence.

Alicia grabbed for another rock and moved a couple of feet sideways. She glanced down. Her party of observers watched, but none had moved.

Her efforts were futile. She knew they'd follow her once she'd covered enough distance. Certainly if she reached the ground, they'd quickly surround her.

She looked up. The walls seemed to touch the clear, blue sky. But small windows cut into the coarse, ivory rock, caught her eye.

Bedchambers maybe? Could she run freely through the castle in prisoner clothes and escape some other way?

She had to risk it. Though by now she wasn't certain her arms would hold out long enough for her to try.

She began to climb upward.

A murmur of conversation ensued. The fae were undoubtedly trying to figure out what she planned now.

"The prisoner is attempting to reach our bedchambers," a woman said, her voice excited. Then she laughed.

Several laughed with the woman.

So the windows did lead to bedchambers.

"You look so serious, Prince Raglan. Do you worry about her?" another female asked.

"I wonder how the woman escaped our prison tower and what she is doing, scaling the cliff side like a monkey. Very queer, don't you think?"

Several chuckled while others uttered agreement.

A monkey? Her blood heated. What would they think if they realized she was a half-fae instead?

"Whatever was she condemned for in the first place?" the prince asked. "Does anyone here know?"

Several said no.

So this Prince Raglan wasn't in charge.

Alicia wondered if he might be intrigued enough with her to keep her out of Queen Irenis's grasp, if Alicia managed to get herself recaptured.

She looked down at the fae, not sure which the prince had been. Several wore gold medallions, but she couldn't make out their symbols.

"What kingdom is this?" she asked.

No one answered her. But several fae's mouths dropped open. Did they think she acted totally rude to address courtiers in such a manner when she was but a lowly prisoner?

To heck with them. She continued her climb upward.

"Why she is heading for your chambers, my prince," a woman

said.

Great. She shifted farther to the right. If she could, she'd find a lady's chambers and borrow one of her gowns. Then she'd attempt to slip past the guards unnoticed.

"No, no, now she's headed for Lady Lucien's chambers."

Laughter resounded.

A lady's chambers. Just what she needed.

But she figured, too, the fae would instantly transport themselves to the lady's chambers, and she'd be apprehended at once.

"Should I inform the guard, Prince Raglan?" a man asked.

"No. This one has been much sport."

Again, she thought of how much the faeries loved to play with the humans. Only this time she assumed they thought she was a fae.

"But if she gets inside—" The man's words were cut short.

Alicia glanced down to see a dark-haired fae wave his hand to silence another.

He must have been Prince Raglan. She stared at him for a moment. Why did he seem so familiar? His dark brown eyes and hair, and his powerful, broad-shoulders and tall stature—all reminded her of someone, but she couldn't make the connection.

She turned her attention back to the climb and inched her way up some more.

Then the prince spoke again. "If she gets into Lady Lucien's chambers, I want a dark fae tracker on hand. Just in case."

"But won't that spoil the chase?" a lady asked.

"I wouldn't want to lose the prisoner before I even find out what onerous crime she's committed."

Well, she hadn't committed any crime before this, but as soon as she could get hold of one of Lady Lucien's gowns, they'd consider her a thief, no doubt. However, they had stolen *her* gowns—Ritasia's rather.

When she reached the ledge, she paused to take a breath. Her arms and legs trembled with the strain of the climb. How was she going to be able to escape this place with a circus of observers watching her every move?

"Why is she hesitating?" a man asked.

No one responded.

Alicia took a deep breath. It was now or never.

She rose on the ledge, then peered in through the window. Lady Lucien's chambers were decorated in robin egg's blue and shimmering gold. Alicia climbed in through the window.

Clapping and cheers from down below followed.

She dashed across the tapestry-carpeted floor and threw a chest open. Then she pulled out a blue gown and golden sandals. Standing, she spied sparkling hair clips decorated in sapphires. And next to these, a golden medallion embossed with the sphinx. Alicia grabbed them, then climbed out of the window. As she expected, the fae had all vanished.

Outside of the room several voices spoke at once.

"Prince Raglan, what are we waiting for?"

Alicia yanked the prison tunic off and tossed it down the cliff. She pulled the fae gown on, then edged closer toward Prince Raglan's bedchambers.

"Oh, she is not here!" a lady exclaimed from Lucien's room.

"Where's the tracker?" the prince shouted.

Alicia tossed the moccasins and shrugged out of the trousers. As they fell to the bottom of the cliff, she climbed in through Prince Raglan's window.

Now all she had to do was hide until the fae sat down for their meal, and she'd attempt her escape.

Voices approached the prince's room.

Alicia glanced around at the black velvet furnishings all embellished with gold. She slid under the bed as the door to the room opened.

"She must have transported, my lord," a man said. "But the tracker should be able to pick up her trail."

"Who was she?" Prince Raglan asked.

Another man said, "A dragon fae. There were two of them who escaped the tower earlier. The one left a trail and a tracker is already after her."

Alicia prayed the countess would not be caught.

"And the other?"

Alicia could only see boots as several men walked into the room.

When there was no response to the prince's question, the prince said, "What about the other?"

"She left no trail."

The prince cursed under his breath. "What fae would leave no trail?"

"A minor, my lord. If she is not yet eighteen…"

"Damn. Then she might not be able to fae-transport. That's why she was scaling our cliffs. Find her! Find her at once!"

"And then?"

"She will tell me who she is."

The men all left the room and closed the door behind them. She assumed faeries didn't normally hide themselves under beds. But then again, they normally wouldn't need to.

She climbed out from under the bed. After slipping the sandals on, she fastened the hair clips to her hair the way Ritasia had done. Finally, she pulled the sphinx medallion over her head.

She was certain she'd be recognized as an imposter at once. But if she were lucky, she could blend in well enough to slip through the halls and leave the castle.

She stood next to the door listening. Voices beyond the door forced a shiver down her spine. When would breakfast be ready? Then she recalled that at Venicia, a bell announced the arrival of the meal.

Before she could crawl back under the bed, the door began to open. The decision was made for her. She dived through the bed curtains and prayed whoever entered the room wouldn't search the prince's bed.

Footsteps crossed the room to the chest. The lid creaked open.

The prince said, "Lady Lucien says her blue gown is missing. The prisoner must have changed clothes. Has anyone found her prison garments yet?"

"No, my lord. You wish to wear the silver tunic for the morning meal?"

There was no response and Alicia imagined the prince had nodded.

"Did anyone discover how we came to have two dragon fae in our prison? We're neutral here. Always have been."

"Spies, my lord. The one was caught at Venicia. They brought her here and Queen Irenis is sending an escort to retrieve her."

"Why was I not told of this?"

"King Persenus has been made aware of the circumstances."

"And the other dragon fae?"

"She was spying on us, my lord. For what reason, we have no idea."

"Did Queen Irenis want this one also?"

"No, my lord."

"Why did she want the other then?"

"Seems, and this is only rumor, my lord, but it seems Prince Deveron has designs on the dragon fae."

Yeah, right. Alicia tried to calm her rapid breathing, fearing the men could hear her heart beating if she didn't cool it.

Silence followed.

Then the prince softly chuckled. "Why would a Denkar royal be interested in a dragon fae? They've hated each other forever."

The man didn't answer.

"Perhaps he has seen her scaling cliffs, too."

"King Persenus wants the girl turned over to Queen Irenis. He doesn't want any trouble with the Denkar."

"What about Morcalon?"

"The dragon fae, King Persenus says, can deal with the Denkar over the matter."

"That's if we find the girl. What is her name?"

"No one bothered to find out, my lord. She's only known as one of the dragon fae."

"All right."

The bells sounded through the castle.

"We will resume our search for the girl after the meal. But I want none to harm her. She'll be great sport following our morning meal."

Alicia narrowed her eyes. If she could, she'd vanish. Show them she wasn't about to be their entertainment for the rest of the day.

"What if she escapes while we're eating?"

"There's no way out for her...not if she can't fae transport. Unless she tries the cliffs again. And she'd never make it climbing in a gown."

She could never have climbed down the cliffs in an hour during the meal either.

When the door shut, she climbed out of the bed.

After crossing the floor, she waited with her ear to the door. When the sound of boots tromping down the hall ceased, she ventured to open the door.

Seeing the hallway clear, she hurried back to Lady Lucien's room. Everyone now knew she wore a blue gown. She would need a different color. She found an emerald green. She slipped into the new gown, then tucked the blue one into the chest. Returning to the dresser where she'd found hairpins, she exchanged the sapphire decorated pins for emerald ones.

And then she left the chambers again.

The castle layout was similar to Venicia. Servants carried platters of partridge on oyster shells into the great hall from the kitchen. Most were too busy to notice her but one caught sight of her, and she figured she was doomed. He appeared to be about fourteen or so, slim of build and not very tall yet. His brown eyes widened at the sight of her.

Yep, she was the escaped dragon fae prisoner all right.

He appeared scared of her, but didn't want to let her out of his sight either. Still, he didn't sound the alarm. Had the green dress confused him? Sure. He looked at the golden medallion encircling her neck.

He must assume she was a noblewoman of the sphinx court, not the prisoner dressed in a stolen green gown.

Alicia smiled her most disarming smile. "Late again, it appears."

He bowed deeply. "My lady."

What now? If she ran for the main doors, he'd sound the alarm. If she walked into the great hall, someone would realize she didn't belong there.

He waited, watching her, holding the tray of food, delaying some courtiers their meal all the while.

She glanced down the hall and saw two very able looking guards standing at a pair of solid oak doors, most likely the main entrance to the castle. They carried lances and watched her, too.

Taking a deep breath, she knew the game had ended.

She might as well make the most of the entertainment, and do the unexpected.

With her head held high, she walked toward the entryway to the great hall.

CHAPTER 16

Deveron joined Prince Raglan at the high table in the great hall, still unsure about Alicia's whereabouts. Raglan had alluded to her being at the sphinx royal castle, but wouldn't say where.

Ritasia, who never bit her nails, was chewing on one with gusto. Micala kept a lookout as they took their seats.

A servant filled Deveron's brass goblet with apple-cinnamon wine as Prince Raglan said to Deveron, "You say you had tracked a Venician guard all the way from Venicia here, who had taken your cousin hostage?"

The smirk on Raglan's lips clued Deveron in that Raglan no more thought Alicia was Deveron's cousin than Ritasia was.

"That's correct. And you say she's a guest here?"

The corner of Raglan's lips twitched and his eyes sparkled with humor. He cleared his throat. "Ahem, yes, a guest."

In King Persenus's dungeon, Deveron presumed. "And she's being brought to the meal, forthwith?"

"She, well, she didn't wish to attend the meal. So I'm sure you can see her sometime afterward."

Ritasia grabbed Deveron's arm and leaned over to speak to him privately. "She just walked into the hall. Over there." She pointed a finger. "The woman wearing the..." She paused, then chuckled. "Wearing the royal sphinx medallion and the green gown."

Deveron rose from his chair. As soon as he did, Raglan stood.

All of the courtiers followed suit.

Raglan quickly motioned to his guards, but Deveron headed to intercept Alicia at the same time. Ritasia and Micala followed on his heels. Raglan hurried to match Deveron's long stride.

"So it appears your cousin did indeed want to eat," Raglan said, his tone amused.

The royal guards had already seized Alicia's arms, but she didn't struggle as Deveron expected her, too. Instead, she tilted her chin up like a determined and stubborn fae would do.

As soon as Alicia saw Deveron stalking toward her, she smiled with such a sunny expression she could have warmed the chilliest day. Certainly, her joyfulness cheered him.

He smiled back, relieved she exhibited such good spirits, but as soon as he could, he had to spirit her away from here. The situation was bound to get ugly.

"Queen Irenis is sending an escort for the lady. May I know her name?" Raglan asked.

Deveron ignored him, realizing the worst…his mother would imprison Alicia next. When he reached Alicia, he said to the guards, "Release the lady at once." He had no intention of being disobeyed and would take every step necessary of freeing Alicia.

The two men looked at Raglan, who motioned for them to do as Deveron ordered.

"What do you intend to do with her?" Raglan asked.

When the guards released her, Alicia wrapped her arms around Deveron and squeezed tightly. "You came for me. You kept your promise."

The great hall grew silent. Deveron hugged her back. "I wanted a rematch. No female fae has ever beaten me at archery. Besides, I haven't figured out how to get even with you for that earlier incident."

She laughed. "Thank you, Deveron." She released him long enough to embrace Ritasia. "And you, too, Ritasia." Then seeing Micala, she said, "What's he doing here? Where's Cassie?"

Worry threaded her words and Deveron wanted to explain what

had happened without Raglan hearing what was going on. He moved her toward the head table.

"Your mother took her home," Deveron said, wrapping his arm around her waist. He led her back to the table.

"What?" Alicia's eyes grew round.

"Your mother came to visit you at South Padre and found Micala with Cassie."

Alicia's shoulders sagged. "What was she told about me? She must be worried sick about my vanishing."

A servant set another plate at the high table.

Deveron took Alicia's hand and squeezed it with reassurance. "She thinks a fae took you. What do you know about your mother?"

He pulled her seat out for her, but she stood staring at him. "Alicia, have you eaten?" He motioned to the chair.

Prince Raglan still stood, and so did the rest of the courtiers. Until the prince sat, no one else could.

Alicia shook her head.

"Then sit and we'll eat and drink for now. We must leave right after the feast."

"So soon?" Raglan took his seat. The rest of the courtiers sat in their seats.

Deveron helped Alicia into hers as she seemed to be in a daze.

"What about my mother?" she whispered.

"She's the dragon fae."

Alicia's lower lip trembled as her eyes watered. She shook her head. "It's not possible. My father is the fae."

He passed a goblet of wine to her as everyone resumed eating, though the conversation remained muted.

Raglan leaned around Deveron and said to Alicia, "We haven't met, young lady. But I'm Prince Raglan and you are?"

"My cousin," Deveron said, buttering a slice of bread. He handed the bread to Alicia.

Raglan smiled at Alicia. "And your cousin's name is?"

"Lady Minxsa," Deveron said.

Raglan chuckled. "I've heard you speak of the lady. But she is of the turtle fae, not the dragon fae. The guard from Venicia distinctly told my father she was a dragon fae."

Alicia whispered to Deveron, "Why would you think my mother is a dragon fae? It's my father who is of the fae."

"Eat, Alicia," Ritasia warned. "Before we have to leave."

"You cannot leave." Raglan folded his arms. "Not unless you tell me what this is all about."

Deveron faced Raglan. "She is a dragon fae. You're right. My mother will want to imprison her because Alicia has distracted me from my duties."

"I hear Queen Irenis wishes you to wed Princess Lorelei."

Deveron gritted his teeth. "It won't come to pass."

"It is rumored you have feelings for the dragon fae."

Alicia's brows rose as if she questioned if this were true or not.

Deveron said to Raglan, "I promised to protect her."

"Ah." Raglan leaned back in his chair. "So that is what you call it. Why do you care so much for her?"

Deveron poked his fork into the dark meat of his fowl. He had no intention of discussing his feelings for Alicia with Raglan or any other.

Raglan said, "She's most entertaining. Wouldn't you say?"

Deveron glanced at Alicia, wondering what she'd done to solicit that remark from Raglan.

She swallowed her bite of food. "I was climbing the cliffs up and down, just for the sphinx fae's benefit. Their accommodations hadn't suited me."

"The dungeon?" Deveron asked. He couldn't help how irritated his voice sounded. He promised to keep Alicia safe, and instead, she ended up in a dungeon, no doubt manacled to prevent her from escaping in the fae way.

"Most unpleasant. The cells could use some good cleaning for one. I thought the sphinx fae were neutral. It seems they are not. Certainly I had committed no crime. And yet here I'm shackled in one of their prison cells."

Deveron looked back at Raglan, waiting for a good response to Alicia's pointed words.

Raglan shrugged and pulled his bird apart with his fingers. "I knew nothing of the two dragon fae females locked in our tower. My father, I was later informed, had the women confined there."

"Where is your father?" Deveron asked, hoping that since he was not at the meal, he was away on a trip and would not cause trouble when Deveron spirited Alicia away from here.

Raglan made a face.

Deveron nodded. "Seeing Princess Zena again."

"Yeah, well, she's too young for him. Barely older than me."

Deveron shook his head. Then he sipped his wine. "I'm taking Alicia from here."

"What will I say happened to her? The courtiers will all know. Your mother's escort will begin to track your trail."

"Will you help us?"

The prince leaned forward and looked at Alicia, who licked butter off her fingers. "I can see why you're attracted to her. But maybe she doesn't want to leave with you, if I could offer her a safe place to stay here."

"I thank you for your offer, Prince Raglan," Alicia said, "but Deveron promises to take me home as soon as he can."

Deveron looked at her, wondering where she ever came up with that notion. Then he realized, he didn't want her to go home at all. His mother would undoubtedly disallow his visits to Alicia in the human world…and though he might venture to see her infrequently, his mother would more than likely put a stop to it. The thought of Alicia being confined in his mother's prison, or worse, instantly came to mind again.

"When we saw her climbing down the cliffs, my first inclination was to call the guards. Instead, we watched the very entertaining young woman to find out what she'd do next. She's very resourceful. I still haven't learned how she got out of the cell in the first place."

Everyone looked at Alicia.

She shrugged. "Fae magic." She smiled when everyone studied

108

her.

Deveron wondered though if perhaps her abilities were starting to appear early. His cousin had already witnessed Alicia's invisibility abilities. What else could she do now?

"Anyway, leave it to say the other dragon fae and I aided one another. I'm not sure she would have aided my escape if she hadn't thought I was a princess though." Again Alicia smiled. Her green eyes sparkled with jollity, but it was her comment that forced Deveron's heart to skip a beat.

"Princess," Ritasia said under her breath.

Deveron stared at Alicia, totally disbelieving what she'd just revealed. "You can't be."

"I know." She chuckled with glee. "Don't look so shocked. I told her she was mistaken."

Raglan cleared his throat. "Jeez, we had one of their royals locked up. And here we're supposed to be neutral. My father will have a conniption."

"You sure did! The countess was pretty perturbed...let me tell you. She'll return to the dragon fae and the word will get out—," Alicia exclaimed.

"A countess?" Raglan's voice had raised a notch. "What was a countess doing spying on us?"

"A spy?" Deveron asked. "What is going on? The royals don't handle such dangerous missions."

"What about Alicia? Was she spying on the Denkar?" Raglan asked.

Alicia raised her brows as she waited for Deveron's response.

The tips of his ears burned. "No. We met under rather unusual circumstances." He couldn't tell Raglan that Alicia was half human. He had no idea what the sphinx fae did to half-fae and half-human creatures.

"Princess," Ritasia said softly, either reminding him of Alicia's importance with the dragon fae, or not believing the young woman could be a princess either.

Alicia might be a princess, but she was still half human. He tapped his knife on the table. "Her mother will go before the dragon fae council. Don't you think?" he asked his sister.

Ritasia sighed deeply. "I don't know. Most fae kingdoms handle matters in a similar manner. But we have no knowledge of dragon fae politics. None of our kind has ever married into their kingdom. If her mother was a princess, this would change the situation significantly. The dragon fae might not have the same kind of loyalty for their own people, especially under the circumstances."

He knew Ritasia was referring to the fact Alicia was half human. If her mother was a royal, but lived apart from her family all of those years, she might not be able to solicit their help now. She might even have been disowned.

"What circumstances?" Raglan asked.

A young boy dashed across the hall and handed a message to Prince Raglan. He read it, then stood abruptly. "The feast ends now."

He grabbed Deveron's arm as he and all of the courtiers stood. "Your mother's escort arrived at the outer gates. I must make arrangements to leave the castle in my father's steward's care. Then I will go with you and Alicia, wherever you intend to take her. I haven't had this much fun in years."

Deveron took a ragged breath. He didn't want Raglan to join their party, especially not if the sphinx prince had some notion he wanted to keep Alicia at his castle, too.

"It's too dangerous. Even Lorelei tried to have Alicia poisoned."

"Tsk, tsk. The lady is a snake." Raglan guided them out of the great hall and down a secret corridor to his father's throne room. "Your mother will undoubtedly not allow you to keep the lady. But maybe my father will permit me to keep her."

Alicia humpfed. "I will not be a kept woman."

The men laughed.

"Most entertaining," Raglan said. "I knew from the moment I saw her, she was a jewel even when wearing the prison uniform."

They stepped inside a large chamber decorated in gold and

green. Three golden thrones took center stage.

Deveron glanced at Alicia's gown. He couldn't deny she appeared beautiful in anything she wore. Even when he had seen her on the beach, covering herself in the baggy T-shirt.

"I'll have to tell the steward to inform your mother's guard that the lady escaped earlier in the day. In truth, she had. And I will tell them, though we tried to have the Denkar tracker her follow her, she had no trail, being that she has not yet reached her majority."

"But then she couldn't fae transport," Deveron reminded him.

"I hadn't thought of that. But Denkar trackers follow fae dust trails, not other kinds of trails. Someone else would have to search for her."

Raglan walked into an anteroom and began speaking to another man.

Deveron took Alicia's hand. "I don't want Raglan to join us."

"We might need others to help us. If Prince Raglan can convince his father I'm no threat to anyone, maybe I can remain here for a time. Maybe even, he could help me to locate my father."

"No."

Her lips parted in surprise. All at once he had an insane overwhelming urge to kiss her. Hell, he was an evil dark fae….or so she said.

He smiled at the notion. So what would an evil dark fae do?

He pressed his lips against hers and pulled her close. "No," he mouthed against her mouth. "*I* promised to keep you safe."

She frowned. "You don't think Raglan will want to keep me permanently. I'm a fascinating diversion. He's not really interested in me."

Ritasia cleared her throat and motioned toward the anteroom with her head.

Raglan stood in the entryway grinning. "Whatever makes you think that, lovely Princess Alicia? Why my father may very well want to make an alliance with your dragon fae kingdom."

Not if he knew she was half-human, he wouldn't, Deveron

surmised.

"So which princess is your mother?" Raglan asked.

Alicia folded her arms. "Not that she is a princess, mind you, but her name is Viviana."

Deveron's heartbeat thundered in his ears.

Ritasia's skin lost its color.

Raglan grinned. "A very rewarding alliance."

CHAPTER 17

Alicia twisted a blond curl of hair between her fingers. "All right. Who do you *think* my mother is?"

"Princess Viviana, of the royal kingdom of Morcalon, daughter of the ruling dragon fae, King Tibero. His only child, I might add," Deveron said.

Alicia looked at Ritasia who nodded. "His *only* child."

"Meaning?" Alicia stood straighter, halfway believing Deveron and the others knew what they were talking about, halfway knowing they were mistaken. Her mother was a human, her father the fae.

"I thought maybe your mother might be a niece. King Tibero has six." Deveron took a ragged breath. "But this changes things."

"How?" Alicia sat down hard on a cushioned forest green chair. She couldn't imagine things could get any worse for her.

"You would be the next in line to take the throne."

"Not when I'm half—"

Deveron's eyes widened and the rich brown color rapidly darkened.

Alicia closed her mouth, stopping what she almost inadvertently said in front of Raglan.

But Raglan noticed Ritasia's and Deveron's concerned expressions. Alicia's unfinished statement further intrigued the sphinx fae. "Half what?" he prompted. His dark eyes shimmered with fascination.

Deveron came to her rescue. "Her mother left the dragon fae

kingdom years ago and for all that time, she has been living in exile…unbeknownst to us."

Raglan's brows rose. "Ah. More intrigue. So who did she run off with?"

"That's what we don't know. Alicia's father disappeared twelve years ago."

Raglan rubbed his chin, then nodded. "So what do we do now?"

Deveron puffed out his chest. "You make up whatever story you need to convince the Denkar escort that the girl has vanished. We will—"

"See my mother." Alicia raised her chin in obstinacy.

"Not at Crislis Castle," Deveron said, matter-of-factly. He didn't appear to be in the mood to change his mind.

"Is that where she would go?" Alicia couldn't squash the worry that if she did go to the castle as the countess bade her to do, Alicia wouldn't find her mother. And the dragon fae would *not* be happy to see Alicia. Would she end up in another dungeon?

"If she wishes help to locate you, I'm sure the princess would to go her father," Deveron said, after thinking on the question for several seconds.

"Then I must go there."

"Ahem," Raglan said, "you can't be seriously thinking of escorting her there. The dragon fae would take you prisoner at once, Deveron."

"I have to go there, don't you think, Deveron? I mean, if my mother convinces her father…" What was Alicia saying? She didn't really believe all of this stuff, did she? Her father had written the journal about the fae. Her father, not her mother. Or did her mother tell him the stories and he wrote them down?

"The dragon fae may go to war over this," Ritasia said, then paused.

"I have the perfect solution." Raglan stiffened his spine. "I will go with you. The dragon fae have nothing against the sphinx as we are neutral in all matters. And perhaps they will see fit to make an alliance with my kind." His lips rose in a silly smirk.

Alicia's heart pounded. Raglan would surely expire on the spot if he knew she was half human.

"I'm not certain your going to Crislis Castle is the best solution," Deveron said to Alicia.

"But your mother couldn't send her people for me there. If I could just see my mother—if she's even at Crislis—she would know what to do."

"You can't take her there," Ritasia finally said. "Raglan's right. The Denkar are the dragon fae's greatest enemy. They would imprison you at once."

"Just like I said." Raglan grinned. "So I will take the princess."

"No. If you insist on going to Crislis, I'll escort you." Deveron took Alicia's hand. "I trust you will get me out of the dungeon if the dragon fae incarcerate me—if it's within your power."

Alicia looked from Deveron's dark expression to Raglan's hopeful one. "You don't think the dragon fae will harm you, Raglan?" She couldn't have Deveron hurt over her.

"Certainly not. I'll take you. We'll see the king and your mother and all will be well."

Deveron pulled Alicia from the chair. "*I* promised to keep you safe." He wrapped his arm around her waist. "I always keep my promises."

"But…," Ritasia said.

It was the last sound Alicia heard before darkness engulfed her. She realized at once—though her mind swirled slightly in confusion—Deveron would endanger his own freedom rather than allow the sphinx fae to assist her alone.

She tilted her chin up to where she thought his face might be and leaned forward to kiss the dark fae. Immediately his warm velvet lips rose in a smile against her mouth. But only for a second. Then he tightened his hold on her and kissed her for all it was worth. She swore she saw a sprinkling of bright lights in the darkness. But she knew she had to be dreaming.

"Alicia," he said. Her name sounded like it drifted on a ribbon of silk, caressing, gentle, and totally sensual.

"Deveron," she said back, scolding, but his kiss deepened, silencing whatever else she meant to say.

She gave in to the swirling blackness, the warmth of his touch, and the feeling that she'd found her soul mate, whether anyone in the fae or human worlds would believe her. *She* believed and that's all that mattered for now.

When the dark began to lighten, she lay beneath a forest of pine, the floor cushioned by orange pine needles, discarded fresh three seasons before. The pine fragrance scented the air, making it smell like it had just received a fresh rain cleansing.

Deveron lay beside her and touched her cheek. "We are not far from Crislis Castle. If you wish to change your mind, however, Alicia—"

"I wish we could sneak in just to see my mother and then take her with us without anyone being aware. But I'm afraid—"

"If wishes only could come true." He sighed deeply, brushing a lock of hair from her cheek. "I will escort you to the gates. But know this. They will arrest me on the spot."

Alicia touched his arm. "They may do the same to me. Maybe we should approach this differently. You wait for me here. I'll attempt to find my mother and return here with her. Then we can leave."

He shook his head.

"But Deveron, listen. If they lock me up, you would be free to come rescue me. What if they lock us both up? Then how would we manage to get free?"

"They would not imprison you."

"No? I'm half human. My mother protected me, if she is who you think she is. Why would she not return to Crislis if she wasn't worried about my safety?" Alicia groaned with a new thought. "You don't think they've imprisoned my mother, do you?"

"Possibly, but only to keep her from leaving again."

"Great." Alicia glanced at a well-worn path leading through the woods nearby. "We won't be able to find out anything if I don't go."

Deveron stood, then pulled her from the ground. She stumbled with dizziness. He slipped his arm around her waist. "Are you going to be all right?"

"Yes, it's the fae travel. I haven't done it for a while."

"We stick together for as long as we can."

"Wait." Alicia touched Deveron's gold lion medallion. "Here, you take the sphinx one I'm wearing. Since they are a neutral fae kingdom, you should be okay."

Deveron felt his medallion. She could tell he didn't want to wear another kingdom's emblem.

"Do it for me, Deveron. They may allow you safe passage. They may want you to leave, but they wouldn't arrest you. Then you'll know how they treat me, too. And whether I'll need rescuing."

He pulled his medallion over his head, then slipped it into his breech's pocket. "The things I do for you."

She smiled and handed him the sphinx medallion. He might have been of the dark fae hunter class, but she'd found a true friend with the fae. "Let's go, before I change my mind."

"We'll walk slowly to give you time."

She chuckled. "I'll walk slowly so I don't collapse. When will I ever get used to fae travel?"

Before either of them could say another word, boots crashed through the underbrush from seemingly every direction, surrounding them.

The predominantly blond male fae appeared, every one of them armed with bows and arrows. Of these, five wore golden medallions embossed with the dragon—dragon fae royalty.

CHAPTER 18

A woman called out amongst the dragon fae as the men quickly surrounded Alicia and Deveron—weapons readied. "She's the one. Princess Alicia. Don't harm her."

Countess Salimina?

Alicia and Deveron stood their ground on the path to Crislis Castle, their hands locked together as if that could save them now.

One of the male royals snickered. "She doesn't look like the princess to me."

"She looks just like her mother, Prince Grotto. And the king will have your head if you harm her," the countess said.

The countess curtsied to Alicia, and she returned the gesture, hoping she'd mastered the gesture with some dignity. "Thank goodness you finally arrived. King Tibero had ordered his soldiers to attack the sphinx castle…" The countess finally seemed to take notice of Deveron. "Who is he?"

"He's my friend, Deveron." Alicia squeezed his hand. "If it were not for him, I wouldn't have ever made it here. I can't fae travel like you can."

The countess's lips parted, then she frowned. "Oh, my heavens. I should have realized you were…" She paused, then said, "Seventeen. Oh…oh…oh, I could have started a war all because I left you behind and…"

Alicia shook her head. "It's all right. Deveron brought me. All is well." If she could get her mother and be out of here, then all would be truly well.

The countess glared at Deveron, which surprised Alicia. Weren't the sphinx fae supposed to be neutral? Then she realized that the sphinx fae had imprisoned both she and the countess. "He had nothing to do with imprisoning us," Alicia quickly said, hoping to dispel the notion that Deveron was their enemy. "And once he found me trying to escape, he aided me."

The countess's expression toward Deveron didn't change. Alicia's skin chilled.

"We must get you inside the castle before anything else goes wrong."

"To see my mother? She is here, right?" If she wasn't, Alicia would have Deveron transport her back to the sphinx castle at once.

"She is."

Alicia breathed a guarded sigh of relief.

"But it is King Tibero who wishes to see you at once, first of all."

The party walked down the path leading to Crislis Castle. Then she had a thought. She turned to Deveron. "Thank you for escorting me here. Maybe I can see you again soon."

"King Tibero will want to thank him personally." The countess's tone of voice was icy.

Alicia tugged at Deveron's hand. Then she whispered in his ear. "Go, Deveron. I fear this will not go well for you, but I must see my mother."

His face remained grim and unyielding. "I have to know what they intend to do with you," he whispered back.

Stubborn dark fae.

They reached the outskirts of the forest and beyond this, a castle loomed, surrounded by a blue stone wall that reached upward more than sixty feet. It nearly blended with the cloudless sky. Flags embossed with the emblem of the golden dragon waved above thirteen towers. All along the guard walk, soldiers dressed in golden tunics watched them approach. Courtiers, too, some of them female, dressed in colorful silky gowns, stood high above, observing the spectacle.

So Alicia served once again as the entertainment for a fae court. Only this time for her own kind…so it would seem. Or at least her fae kind half.

She held her head high as the countess walked on one side of her and Deveron stayed on her right side. He held on tightly to her hand and she envisioned he not only wished to comfort her—certainly she felt distressed—but also might have the notion to transport her away from harm if need be.

She imagined the dragon fae would not like to see her friendship with any fae that was not dragon at the moment however.

The countess motioned to the blond haired, green-eyed man who had said Alicia didn't look like the princess as he led the cavalcade. "Prince Grotto is your cousin, once removed, Princess Alicia. One of your mother's aunts' sons."

Before this, Alicia had thought her mother was an only child…and she learned she was, but she also never thought she had any uncles or aunts…and therefore no cousins, removed or otherwise.

The countess added, "He was the next in line to inherit the throne until your mother returned. Now you are."

Right. As soon as…

Or did the king, her grandfather, already know she was half human? He had to. That's undoubtedly why her mother had run away from home.

And here to think Alicia believed only her father had run away from them. Who would have thought her mother had left her own family? Because she fell in love with a human. But why hadn't her mother returned home with Alicia when her father abandoned them?

A sickening feeling worked its way into the pit of Alicia's stomach. Her grandfather wouldn't wish to welcome Alicia since she was half fae. Maybe her grandfather had changed his mind after her mother had been gone for so many years.

Still, Alicia couldn't shake the feeling that she was now being escorted into the Roman legions arena where a lion would soon attack her and chew her to pieces.

Guards stood on either side of the gates to the castle, pointing their lances forward as if in salute.

But as soon as Alicia and her escort stepped inside the courtyard, guards rushed forth to close the gates. Just as quickly, others bolted out of the guardhouse, carrying shackles.

"Go, Deveron!" Alicia shouted, her heart tripping with fear.

"I promised to protect you." Before he could transport her, two guards yanked him away from her, breaking their physical contact.

She assumed he was trying to take her from there, but couldn't in time, and then, though he could have still managed to save himself, he stayed for her sake.

She fought the tears that welled up in her eyes. Angered he wouldn't leave, then try to come back for her, she slugged one of the guards who snapped the special manacles over Deveron's wrists.

The guards began to drag him toward one of the towers as two others grabbed her wrists, pulling her away from him. "No!" Alicia screamed. "He brought me here. Free him at once! Without his aid, I'd still be at the sphinx castle."

Her words fell on deaf ears. Some smiled at her comments, others frowned.

Grotto motioned to another guard. "Go ahead and manacle her, too."

"No," the countess said, blocking the guard's path, who took a step in Alicia's direction. "She's underage. She can't fae transport."

So Alicia was to be a prisoner.

The countess spoke to Alicia next. "Come. I'll take you to my chambers where you can wash, tidy up a bit, and then I'll escort you to see King Tibero."

"With a guard escort," Grotto said.

The countess glared at him.

Alicia watched the direction the guards took Deveron, the northernmost tower. Somehow she had to see her mother. Maybe she could help Alicia to free Deveron. He glanced back at her before the guards shoved him inside the tower. She lunged after him, dragging her own guards a step or two before they had her under control. Her heart sank to see him shackled and roughly treated especially when she had been the cause of it. And now she felt useless to help him...for the moment.

"What about my mother?"

The countess guided her across the courtyard and into the main entrance of the castle. She led her into a hall and up a broad flight of stairs next. "I'm certain you'll get to see your mother at the nooning meal."

"But she's wearing a retaining collar," Grotto said, following behind them. "To think the king's only child would have to be prevented from using her fae magic to escape her kingdom again. And to think the king still has a soft spot for her even after she disobeyed him and married the sphinx fae."

Alicia stumbled on the stairs as her heart nearly gave out. Her father was a sphinx fae?

The guards tried to lift her, but Alicia's legs had turned to rubber again, and she collapsed, unable to go any further.

"What's wrong?" the countess asked. "Your face is as white as the full moon. Oh was it the fae transport that unsettled you so?"

Alicia didn't want to discuss her father in front of Prince Grotto, not when he was obviously angry with her for turning up at Crislis Castle and ruining his chance at ruling the kingdom. Though she doubted the king had it in mind that she would rule in his place when the time came.

Her head swirled with confusion. She knew her father was a fae. But she'd never guessed her mother was also. Now that meant she wasn't even half human?

"Princess?" the countess said, trying to help her up.

Alicia's stomach revolted. "I'm going to be sick."

"Carry her to my bedchambers," the countess ordered one of the guards.

The man lifted Alicia off the stairs and carried her the rest of the way up and then down the hall.

Tapestries of dragons and dragon fae hung against the stone walls. A gold carpet ran the length of the hall. And from the ceiling, crystal chandeliers lighted their way.

"You look awfully pale," the countess said as she ran her hand over Alicia's arm. She motioned to another guard. "Tell the king Princess Alicia is unwell. We may take a bit longer to see him."

"Yes, countess," the man said, then stalked back down the hall to the stairs.

"She is faking it," Grotto said.

"Her cheeks have lost their color and her skin shimmers with a faint perspiration. Even a fully-grown fae cannot fake those kinds of symptoms."

She preceded Alicia into her bedchambers. "Lay her on my bed."

Everything was decorated in peach and forest green. But the thing that caught Alicia's eye was a statue of a peach-colored flamingo, sitting four feet high in a corner of the room.

The countess smiled. "Something I picked up on a visit to the human's world."

She waved her fingers at the five men who had escorted them. "You are dismissed."

Prince Grotto countermanded her order. "Sir Trenton, you will stay with Princess Alicia at all times."

"Outside of my bedchambers," the countess insisted. "The lady will wear one of my favorite gowns. So if you would, Prince Grotto and Sir Trenton…"

The prince glared at Alicia. "You won't leave here, unless the king wishes it. Do you understand?"

"Deveron must be released at once! He brought me here. He didn't harm me. You have no right throwing him in a cell," Alicia said, her voice hot with anger.

Grotto's lips turned up into a wicked smile. "And what if history repeats itself? What if you were to run off with this sphinx fae and abandon your kingdom?"

"Then you would rule, wouldn't you?"

A flicker of interest seemed to flash across his green eyes. Then he snarled. "You will not leave. And the sphinx fae will never have you."

"Where do you come up with such an unfounded assumption? He brought me here. If he wanted to keep me, he would never have come into a pit full of poisonous vipers such as yourself."

Grotto grinned. "That's what your family is to you? And you're to rule us some day? King Tibero must change his ruling or all will be lost." He stormed out of the room with the guard on his heel.

As soon as the guard shut the door, the countess pulled a burgundy gown from her chest. "It would be wise not to rile him, Princess. He has been horrible to live with since your mother returned."

"Where is my mother?"

"Locked in her bedchambers. But word will be sent to her at once that you are safely here now. She was extremely distraught to hear the sphinx fae had imprisoned you and that they had every intention of turning you over to the Denkar, no less."

"My father. You can't be serious that he is a sphinx fae."

"Yes. The king was furious when she eloped with your father. They'd tried to get permission from King Tibero and from his parents as well. None of them would hear of it. I don't think any of them realized how stubborn your parents could be. But so were their families. King Tibero wouldn't have Princess Viviana returned here by force no matter what, though his advisors advised him to.

"Then she came here looking for you, frantic that a fae kingdom—she thought her own kind—had taken you away. When she discovered we weren't the ones who had stolen you, it was too late. Spies like me…" Viviana grinned. "Well, we set out on our own to try to find out which kingdom held you hostage. Only I wasn't very good at the job and got myself thrown into the prison quickly enough. You can't imagine my delight in seeing you in the cell next to mine."

Alicia sat up on the bed, her stomach settling.

"Why can't I see her, before I see my grandfather?"

"The king has said he doesn't want her unduly influencing you. She told him you knew nothing about your fae heritage."

"No, nothing."

"He realized you are not at fault for your mother's transgressions."

"She loved my father," Alicia said, furious that her grandfather would be so cruel.

The countess helped her off the bed and out of her gown. "Yes, but in the end, he couldn't stay with her."

"Why?"

"His own people forced him to choose. They threatened to kill you and your mother if he didn't leave and do as they said."

"So he did leave us to protect us."

The countess slipped the burgundy gown over Alicia's head. "Yes. But your mother feared telling you. She worried you'd search for him. She wasn't sure how the sphinx fae would treat you."

"I thought he was the fae and my mother human."

The countess's eyes grew big, then she laughed out loud. "Human? Now that's truly funny."

Alicia didn't think so. As far as she knew, that's just what she'd been all these years. Being a fae seemed funny...not as in humorous, but odd.

"Well, I do suppose it would seem that way. Most of your fae abilities don't kick in until you turn eighteen." The countess replaced the emerald hair clips in Alicia's hair with diamond decorated ones. Then she lifted a dragon medallion off her dresser. Slipping it over Alicia's head, the countess said with much feeling, "Now you are officially a royal dragon fae."

She patted Alicia's shoulder. "Do you feel all right to see the king now?"

No. Alicia wasn't sure she'd ever feel all right about that. Not when her grandfather tried to stop her mother from marrying the man she loved. Fae rather.

TERRY SPEAR

"What about my father? I didn't see him at the sphinx castle."

The countess opened her bedchamber's door. "That's because his older brother is the king of the sphinx fae. Your father married the Venician queen."

Lorelei's my stepsister?

Alicia didn't hear anything more as her temple swirled with bewilderment, and her world instantly faded to midnight.

CHAPTER 19

The countess called to the guard as Alicia came to on the floor of her chambers. "Help me with the princess!"

Alicia's mind could barely focus. How could her father have married the Venician queen? And worse—that horrible Lorelei and Phillinois were her half-sister and brother? Or were they stepsister and brother? Maybe the queen had had the children by another fae. And Alicia wasn't truly related to the devil fae.

She frowned as the guard lifted her, then carried her across the floor. How could her father have abandoned her mother and her, then married another woman?

As soon as she was resting on the mattress, the countess said, "Sir Kendall, inform the king, Princess Alicia is too unwell to see him at the moment. And get the physician for the lady."

"But Prince Grotto said—"

"The lady is indisposed. Do you think she'll fight me to get away?"

"No, countess. But Prince Grotto ordered me to stay here to guard her and—"

The countess drew herself up and lowered her voice to a harsh roar. "If the princess grows more ill, the king will have your head! Prince Grotto doesn't know how poorly she's feeling. Now go."

Still he hesitated, glancing from Alicia to the countess again.

"Go!"

He grumbled under his breath and left the room.

The countess returned to the bed and patted Alicia's hand. "Are you feeling nauseous?"

Alicia swallowed hard. "I never knew what had happened to my father. How could he have left my mother like he did? To marry another woman?"

"Under threat of his family having you and your mother killed, he really had no choice."

Alicia fought shedding a tear as her eyes misted.

"Is that what's making you ill?" the countess asked. "The news about your father?"

"He never came back to see us. Never."

The countess smiled. "I imagine he found a way to see your mother and how you were doing over the years. The fae have magic you are probably unaware of."

"But he married—"

"Sometimes we must do what we don't like. As royals, it's expected of us."

"Are you married?"

"By heavens no. Though I am betrothed. But it'll be another year before I have to marry the duke. Now that you are here with us, the king will decide on a husband for you."

Alicia's stomach had been settling, but the nausea returned.

"Oh, your cheeks have lost their color again. Forgive me. I shouldn't have brought it up." The countess grabbed a peach feathered fan and waved it in front of Alicia's face.

Then a knock on the door disturbed the peace.

"Come in," the countess hollered.

A man, whose blond hair was streaked with white, entered the room. A red velvet cloak draped over his shoulders, fastened with a gold chain. And instead of a tunic like the other men wore, he wore a long shift-like gown of purple that reached gold sandaled feet.

Behind him a white-haired man entered the chambers.

"This is my granddaughter?" the first man said.

This was the king?

* * *

Deveron paced across the cell in the Crislis Castle's tower, hoping the king was treating Alicia with respect. When Prince Grotto had told the guard to shackle her, Deveron had turned with every intention of protecting her. But luckily, the countess stepped in to aid Alicia.

Would the countess also help Alicia to free him, or did her loyalty only extend to aiding the royal princess, granddaughter of the king?

The chains linking his manacles clinked as he crossed the floor back and forth. At least they hadn't manacled him to the wall.

But how could he escape without Alicia's help? His mother would have a fit. She wouldn't hesitate to wage war against the dragon fae if she learned they had imprisoned him.

A key ground in the lock to the cell door, then a guard shoved the door open.

His stomach clenched.

The guard walked into the room followed by Prince Grotto.

Time for the interrogation?

The prince walked around Deveron in a tight circle, examining him from head to foot. "What are you to the princess?"

"A friend when she needed one."

"Did you take her from South Padre Island?"

Deveron's lips thinned. If he told Prince Grotto he had taken Alicia from the Island, he'd have to say why. If he told the prince he was attempting to keep her out of his mother's grasp, the prince would want to know who his mother was. Then, the prince would know Deveron was not a sphinx fae, but a lion fae—the crown prince in fact, of the Denkar.

"You took her from South Padre Island?" Grotto repeated. "Her mother said a fae witness told her enough that she assumed a fae had taken Alicia. Since you were with her last…"

"You assume *I* was the fae."

"Do you deny it?" Grotto folded his arms and narrowed his sharp green eyes.

Deveron could see a slight family resemblance between Grotto and Alicia when she had appeared angry.

"I did."

"For what reason? And speak carefully. I will know if you're lying."

Because the prince already had his mind made up as to the reason, Deveron assumed.

"I'm not of the sphinx fae," Deveron said.

Grotto glanced at the royal sphinx medallion encircling Deveron's neck.

Deveron explained, "I'm lion fae." Before the prince could close his gaping mouth, Deveron added, "The *crown prince* of the Denkar."

Grotto stared at him, not uttering a sound.

"If my mother learns you have imprisoned me, she won't hesitate to wage war with your people."

The dragon fae ignored the importance of Deveron's words. "Why did you take Alicia from South Padre? Surely you realize your actions could have provoked the same response from our kingdom."

Now for the tricky part. Alicia's people had to know that she was half human, so there would be no secret in that. He would explain the truth of the matter. "My mother assumed Alicia was half human."

Grotto's eyes widened, and he opened his mouth to speak, then clamped it shut.

"My mother had no idea that Alicia was half dragon fae. It is the human part that would have disturbed her, particularly when I became interested in Alicia. As for myself, I never gave her fae heritage any thought. She didn't know which fae she came from."

Grotto looked at the floor for a moment, then looked back at Deveron. "If you have lied about who you are, it will not go well for you." He started toward the door, then stopped and turned. "What did you mean that you're interested in Alicia?"

"She's a remarkable fae." Deveron couldn't help smiling.

Grotto scowled. "The king will not be pleased." He stalked out of the cell.

* * *

In the countess's bedchambers, the king's luminescent green eyes sparkled with interest while his lips quirked into a smile as he observed Alicia. Dimples punctuated his tanned cheeks. "She looks just like her mother did at that age."

"It is indeed Princess Alicia," the countess said.

"What ails you child?" he asked.

Alicia assumed mentioning the upset over her father wouldn't set well with the king. He probably wouldn't want to hear anything about the man who stole her mother's heart, then encouraged her to run away.

"She's only now learned about her father," the countess said.

The king's cheeks darkened.

The other man poured a powder into a goblet filled with wine, then handed it to Alicia. "Drink this and it'll settle your stomach."

She noticed then the guard standing in the doorway. Would he make her drink the concoction if she refused?

"Drink, dear Alicia. Afterward, I will have your mother brought to you."

Under guard? Like Alicia was being guarded?

If the king felt any compassion toward her, could she get Deveron released? "A sphinx fae, Deveron, brought me here. He's being held in your dungeon. Will you release him?"

Again the king's face grew stormy. "*He* is my enemy." He began to pace. "No, I will not release him until I know the reason for his being here."

Then she realized the difficulty. Her grandfather most likely hated the sphinx for the one taking her mother away from him. Would it help to tell the king, Deveron was really the crown prince of Denkar? That if his mother learned the dragon fae held Deveron prisoner, she probably wouldn't hesitate to wage war with them?

"Your Majesty," Alicia began carefully.

"Kingship," the countess corrected her. "Your Majesty is a

131

human term."

"Drink the medicinal wine," the other man said.

"The doctor knows best," the king added.

Alicia hoped it wasn't drugged to keep her complacent. She sipped the drink. It tasted like wine and a hint of cinnamon and tingled on her tongue.

"Call for her mother," the king said to the countess.

She smiled at Alicia, then curtseyed to the king and left the room.

"Drink," the doctor coaxed.

The concoction warmed her throat all the way down to her stomach.

"About Deveron…"

The king shook his head. "I will not speak about the prisoner again until Prince Grotto has had a chance to talk to him."

Would they treat him badly? Torture him? She gritted her teeth, hoping she could change her grandfather's stubborn mind.

Before she could worry about it further, rapid footsteps grew closer to the bedchambers. The countess said, "Oh yes, Princess Viviana, she cannot wait to see you."

When Viviana stepped into the room, Alicia nearly fell out of the bed to reach her. Her mother looked so different, dressed in the fae gowns of powder blue silk, her blond hair piled high on her head in an elegant hairstyle. Her green eyes were blurry and her cheeks glistened with fresh tears.

They hugged and kissed as everyone else in the room remained deathly quiet.

"Alicia, I worried so for you. I should have returned you here long ago. I should have told you about our heritage. Can you ever forgive me?"

"You wanted to protect me. You only did what you thought best." Alicia hugged her mother again, wanting her mother to know she felt nothing but gladness to be with her again. Then she touched the golden collar encircling her mother's neck. Though it looked like a piece of elegant jewelry, she figured her mother would feel ashamed to have to wear the retaining collar, prohibiting her from conducting any fae magic. "Is this really necessary?" She looked at the king.

"It remains until I'm assured the two of you are not leaving here."

"I promise I'll stay." Alicia assumed it was her grandfather's greatest wish. She couldn't help but be pleased to find she had more family. Especially one so exalted as her grandfather, king of the dragon fae. And the notion she could be queen…

She smiled.

Then she tried to win Deveron's freedom again. "But, Your Kingship, my friend has been unjustly imprisoned in your dungeon. He must be released at once."

Prince Grotto rushed into the chambers, then quickly bowed to the king. "He's the crown prince of the Denkar, Your Kingship. Prince Deveron is the one we now have imprisoned in our dungeon."

The king shifted his attention to Alicia. "I thought you said he was of the sphinx fae. Is this true? That's he's of the Denkar?"

"Yes, it is," she said. Though she meant for her words to be stronger, they sounded incredibly meek. Would they kill him?

She couldn't allow it.

"What were his intentions toward my granddaughter?" the king asked Grotto, as if the prince would know better than Alicia.

On the other hand, he might not believe her. She spoke first anyway. "Only honorable. I asked him to bring me here to find my mother. He did so even though he knew he'd be imprisoned. I had no other means of getting here. I tried to get him to leave without me, but he feared for my safety."

Her grandfather frowned. "With your own kind?"

"He vowed to protect me always. He had made a promise."

The king rubbed his chin.

"Oh, Alicia," her mother said under her breath, her voice filled with sadness. "What have you done?"

What had she done? She had done nothing! But found her

mother and…and…

The king looked at Viviana, then said, "Everyone leave the room but my daughter and granddaughter."

As soon as everyone vacated the chambers and the guard shut the door on their exodus, the king turned to Alicia. "History seems to be repeating itself." His tone was grim.

Her mother said, "You must wed whosoever your elders—in this case your grandfather and the parents of the male fae—deem fit. Don't make the same mistake I made, Alicia."

Alicia couldn't believe her mother's words. Did she not love her father any longer?

"You mean that I am a mistake?" Alicia asked, her brows deeply furrowed as she nearly growled the words.

CHAPTER 20

A resounding repeated banging at the countess's chamber's door forced King Tibero to shout, "Who is interrupting me now?"

The door opened only enough for a man to poke his nose in. "My lord, a woman, claiming to be the princess of the Denkar, and a man, claiming to be the prince of the sphinx fae, have come seeking Prince Deveron's release. The woman says he is her brother, and her mother, Queen Irenis, is being made aware that we have taken him prisoner."

Alicia folded her arms. "Just what I'd said, if anybody would bother to listen to me." And to think someday she'd rule the place. She'd certainly make some great changes.

Before the king could say a word, another man leaned in through the doorway, opening it wider. "Sire, six Denkar fae have just arrived at our gates. They say their crown prince is here, and they demand to see him at once."

The king's chest rose as he filled his lungs with air, then answered. "The afternoon feast is nearly served. See that these *guests* are taken to my solar. Have Lord Jessup provide wine for them until the bells ring for the meal."

"And the prisoner?"

The king ground his teeth as he looked at Alicia. She attempted her most pleading, woeful look. It almost always worked with her mother.

His hard face softened.

She curbed smiling, not wanting to risk him changing his mind.

"Take him to my throne room. But remove the shackles first. Tell him he will have an audience with me before the meal. That he has nothing to fear. After feasting with us, he's free to leave."

"Can I go to him, too?" Alicia asked, trying to hide the enthusiasm in her voice in case it irritated her grandfather.

"No." He motioned to his men. "Go, do as I say."

When the men closed the door, the king shook his head as he gazed at Alicia. "You are just like my daughter when she was your age."

Then he stalked out of the room. He turned to Viviana. "Return to your chambers until…" Then he reconsidered. "Join me in my throne room with my granddaughter."

Within minutes, the king sat on a golden throne, encrusted with gems of every conceivable color. A long blue runner led to the dais where the two thrones sat. The other was just as ornate, just as decorated, but vacant.

He patted on the empty seat and wiggled his finger at Alicia. She whispered to her mother, "Why don't you take the seat there?"

"He is punishing me for running away. It won't always be like this and when you are queen, you will treat me well."

"But you should sit upon the throne."

"Go, before my father throws a tantrum."

Alicia smiled, not imagining an old man could do such a thing. Then she reconsidered. A king throwing a tantrum could be an awful situation for the ones he ruled. She hugged her mother, then walked down the carpet. The throne room soon filled up with courtiers, the ones dressed in the most elaborate gowns and tunics most likely the higher lords and ladies made their way to the front of the crowd.

Guards escorted Ritasia, Raglan and the fae trackers in through a side entrance. Alicia's heart skipped to see Ritasia.

The princess's face remained stern and unsmiling. Alicia assumed it was because she still feared for her brother.

Then guards led Deveron before the king, dressed in new garments of red satin, heavily embroidered in gold.

Alicia wanted to rush to him, to embrace him, kiss him, and tell him how worried she'd been about him. But something in her reaction to seeing him, caused the king to motion to one of his lords.

The tall man hurried forth, and took her arm, then guided her to stand before the king. She curtseyed.

He smiled. Then his face turned harsh. He motioned for her to sit beside him.

She glanced back at Deveron. An almost imperceptible smile played on his lips and in his dark brown eyes. Most would probably not recognize it for what it was, but she knew. Not only was he relieved she had come to no harm, he seemed to be glad she was being seated at the king's side. But something more?

Did he think her grandfather was making some momentous overture by welcoming the prince of the Denkar into his throne room? She sat down on the throne and smiled a Deveron.

He smiled brightly.

The king was not amused. He cleared his throat. "We thank you for bringing our future queen back to us, Prince Deveron, crown prince of the Denkar."

Movement near the entryway caused a low roar of conversation, and the king paused.

A guard rushed forth, bowed hastily before the king, then spoke low for only the king and close courtiers to hear. "Sire, Queen Irenis is here with a force of too many to fathom."

"Show her in. Tell her to join us for our feast."

Again the courtiers conversed in a hushed roar as events unfolded.

Ritasia watched the entryway for her mother's arrival, if her mother dared enter the dragon's lair. But Deveron kept his gaze focused on Alicia. Her cheeks burned with embarrassment.

Was he trying to make a statement to the king? That he wanted the dragon fae princess and she him?

She couldn't deny she was totally attracted to him, but she had a whole new life to become accustomed to.

To heck with that. She wanted to see more of Deveron. That's what she wanted to become accustomed to…more of the same life with the dark fae hunter.

His smile broadened.

And he knew it, too.

Damn him.

Was she so transparent when it came to her feelings for him?

Yeah.

And then boots tromped toward the throne room. Two guards led the way, several more followed as a dark haired female fae walked in between them. She held her head high as her dark eyes surveyed the attendees, her eyes shifting from her son, who didn't bother to look in her direction, and Ritasia. Seeing her children well, the queen glanced at Alicia, then cocked a dark brow.

Yep, Alicia was the cause of the trouble for all their kingdoms.

Alicia smiled at the queen, dressed in flowing gowns of purple. The queen never smiled, but shifted her attention to the king.

He eyed her with a darkness that disturbed Alicia. They wouldn't fight, would they?

Then what? She'd want to side with Deveron and Ritasia…but her mother. She took a deep breath, trying to massage her jagged nerves. She couldn't upset her mother.

The king stood and bowed.

The queen curtseyed most regally.

There seemed to be a deep sigh that spread across the breadth of the throne room. Did everyone think as she did? That war was imminent?

"Welcome to Crislis," the king said, still standing.

Alicia rose to her feet, realizing belatedly she should have been standing once he stood. She had a lot to learn about royal court proceedings.

She caught Deveron's eye. He immediately winked at her and grinned.

The queen noticed their reaction at once and stiffened her spine.

138

The king said, "We would be honored if you would join us at a feast to welcome my granddaughter and my daughter home."

"I would be delighted," the queen said, her voice icy.

"It seems, Queen Irenis, I have rather a situation on my hands." He stepped down the stairs and reached his arm out to her.

Alicia stared at the king's actions. He was going to escort his worst enemy to the meal?

The queen rested her hand on his arm, and they walked down the carpeted path toward the entryway.

Immediately, Deveron dashed forth to take Alicia's arm.

"Oh, Deveron, are you all right? They didn't torture you or…"

He kissed her, stopping her words at once.

A pronounced number of gasps resounded across the room.

No one left the room, not until the king and other royal family members exited. So Alicia's face burned with a fever of embarrassment that Deveron would kiss her in front of her mother, and his sister, and the whole dragon fae court.

What would her grandfather think? Would he lock Deveron in chains again?

She peeked around Deveron's arm.

Her grandfather and Deveron's mother were watching them. And then her grandfather shook his head, and the lady looked at him. The two walked outside of the throne room in conversation.

Alicia's mother and her ladies hurried after the king. And Deveron followed with Alicia.

Raglan escorted Ritasia after them. When Alicia looked back at Ritasia, she shook her head, too.

Well, Alicia was certain she'd hear more from both her mother and grandfather about her poor manners after the meal.

But just after everyone was settled into their chairs at the high table, a messenger brought word to the king. He looked at Viviana, then at Alicia. And again he shook his head.

Now what had happened? The suspense was killing Alicia as the king motioned for the man to leave.

Loud voices and the tromping of more boots nearing the great hall caused everyone in the hall to cease their conversation.

CHAPTER 21

As soon as the gray-haired man entered the hall, Deveron knew him to be Raglan's father. No doubt upset with his son's visiting the dragon fae, particularly after imprisoning two of their royals, he was sure to worry Raglan might have been incarcerated.

King Persenus approached the table, acknowledging first that his son was all right, then greeted the dragon fae king and smiled broadly at the lion fae queen. But the next man who entered the hall forced Alicia to rise from her chair.

What was going on? Did King Reynolds learn Deveron was interested in Alicia and not his daughter, Lorelei? Great. Now he had to explain himself out of this situation.

King Reynolds's gaze shifted from Alicia to her mother, and Deveron could see a flame burned for Alicia's mother.

Alicia folded her arms and scowled at King Reynolds.

She couldn't be his daughter. She was half human. Wasn't she?

Deveron nudged at her arm, trying to get her to sit down beside him again.

But instead, she stepped away from her chair and stalked toward King Reynolds. "How could you leave us like you did? And mother? How could you come here and show your face when you married that despicable...despicable..."

Deveron joined her, hoping to make a new marriage proposal at once while the time was ripe. He couldn't believe his good fortune, or

141

Ritasia's that King Reynolds was Alicia's father. He bowed to King Reynolds and said, "My mother has attempted to make an alliance between my kingdom and yours. I wonder if you would wish to still make this…only Alicia would be my bride?"

Alicia's father's mouth dropped as he looked from Deveron to Alicia. Then he frowned. "This would have to be decided by—"

"I wholeheartedly agree to the arrangement," Queen Irenis chimed in.

And why not? Not only would his mother be allied with the sphinx, and it appeared Alicia was next in line to the Venician throne by virtue of being King Reynolds's first child, but also an alliance would be forged with the dragon fae. Would King Tibero agree also to the proposal?

Deveron waited with baited breath. Say yes, King Tibero. Say yes.

The king looked at Viviana who nodded her consent.

Alicia's mother was agreeable. Now if only the king would agree…

Queen Irenis tapped her fingers on the table as she waited for King Tibero to announce his decision.

He nodded.

Deveron smiled, but Alicia did not.

She wasn't interested? His blood heated. She would turn down the crown prince of the lion fae?

"Nobody asked me," Alicia said, her chin tilted upward, her lips pressed firmly together in the cutest little pout.

"Would you agree?"

"I…"

"Not for another year," King Tibero said. "She doesn't come of age until then. She cannot make a decision of this magnitude before then."

Viviana seemed to take a deep breath of relief.

"Nonsense," Queen Irenis said. "She is not the one to make the decision. Her elders have made the decision for her."

"A year," the king reiterated.

"I will make sure you don't change your mind during the year," Deveron said, kissing Alicia's hand.

"Without seeing the young man," the king added.

"What?" Queen Irenis squeaked. "You can see they're clearly in love. They're meant to be together."

His mother didn't care about things like that. She wanted commitment and feared during the year, politics might change the scheme of things as they now stood. What if King Tibero decided to marry his granddaughter off to someone else? Was this the reason for his agreeing to the marriage, only to revoke the plans by the end of the year? Would he have other suitors chase after Alicia, wearing her down until she felt she loved one of them instead, particularly as she wouldn't see Deveron in so long? Maybe her feelings for him would fade with time?

He smiled and led Alicia back to her seat. He had no intention of staying away from her. No intention whatsoever. Another dark fae quality. Extreme perseverance…when it was something one wanted badly enough.

When they sat together, she glanced over at her father who sat next to her mother. Alicia's grandfather didn't seem pleased, but Viviana did.

They talked in whispered secrets and laughed and touched with fond remembrances. Good thing his Venician wife didn't see him flirting with his former dragon fae wife.

Deveron handed Alicia a slice of bread. "You won't forget me during the year, will you?"

"How could I ever forget you, Deveron?"

"Time has a way of making memories fade," he said glumly.

She smiled. "Somehow I can't see how it would be possible. Do you fear I might find someone else more appealing in that time?"

"No." He couldn't look her in the eyes or she'd see he was lying.

"Liar. You do, too. Do you think I'm that fickle?"

"I worry your grandfather may use this as a time to find someone

143

more of his choosing to court you."

"I won't see anyone."

He smiled. "But me."

"Not even you, so my grandfather says." She reached over and touched his hand.

He wrapped his fingers around hers. "To think I thought you were half human."

"You couldn't have been more surprised than me."

"You know a cousin of mine saw you turn invisible."

"I did?"

He nodded, then smiled. "As soon as you can fae transport we can secretly rendezvous," he whispered.

"You may disobey your mother all of the time, but I don't mine."

He buttered a slice of bread, totally amused with Alicia. "When you have not had my kisses for so long, you will find a way to see me."

"I will obey my grandfather. What if he said I couldn't marry you, if I saw you behind his back? No," she said lifting her goblet off the table, "it wouldn't do to anger him."

She glanced at her father. "He looks just like I remember him, only a little grayer. And he loves my mother still. I don't want us to have to steal moments like that, if my grandfather should say no to my marrying you in the end."

"I would pine away for a year if I could not see you for all of that time."

She twisted her mouth in thought. "I could see Ritasia."

"What?"

"Sure, I could visit Ritasia, and then if you happen to be with her at the time—"

"That's my faery princess.

"If my grandfather will permit it."

"You promised you'd teach Ritasia how to practice with a bow."

"Ah, I did."

"And I want a rematch."

"You'll never beat me." She grinned at him.

144

He wanted to kiss her smiling lips again, but caught her grandfather's concerned eye. "We will just have to find a place to make it happen. Neutral grounds, so to speak."

"To neutral grounds," she said, raising her goblet to his.

But when the feast was done, the king ensured Deveron was smartly escorted out of the hall after barely giving Alicia a quick peck on the lips.

Alicia gave her father a warm hug. "I would come visit you at Venicia, but Lorelei tried to poison me and had me imprisoned in the sphinx's dungeon."

"You may visit me anytime, Alicia. I will let your sister and brother know how displeased I was with their actions toward you. And they will also know what would become of them should they try anything more when you visit."

Queen Irenis gave Alicia a strange little smile. "You know my son I believe almost as well as I do. And I approve."

Alicia wasn't sure what the cryptic message meant, but she thought it might have something to do with her son disobeying orders, only this time it benefited Queen Irenis. In fact, the last time it had, too.

Queen Irenis kissed her cheeks, then hurried after Deveron.

"We must get together to practice archery," Alicia said to Ritasia next.

"Oh, yes." She glanced back in the direction of her disappearing mother. "You know what my mother meant, don't you?"

Alicia took Ritasia's hands and leaned over and whispered in her ear, "Deveron wishes to see me despite my grandfather's orders."

Ritasia's broad smile indicated Alicia had guessed right. "Archery, yes. And I will help you in any way that I can."

She hugged Alicia, then hurried after her mother.

King Persenus said to Alicia, "I'm your father's brother, and therefore your uncle. Do not be a stranger to our kingdom. You are always welcome."

Prince Raglan chimed in, "And I'm your cousin, disappointedly."

When the rest of the royal guests had taken their leave, Alicia met with her grandfather and mother in his solar.

"Are you happy about the arrangements with Prince Deveron?" the king said, taking a seat on a well-cushioned golden chair.

Alicia knelt before him. "Very. It will be all right with you if I visit with Princess Ritasia to help her to improve her archery skills? She is most awful at it."

He smiled. "Yes, but she will never be as good at it as a female dragon fae archer."

"No, but anything would be an improvement." She took a deep breath, thinking about how she'd never return to her human world again. But she couldn't leave things as they were without saying goodbye to Cassie. "One other thing, if it pleases you. Can I return to finish my vacation on South Padre Island with my friend, Cassie?"

"The human girl?" Her grandfather wrinkled his brow. "I don't want you to see any more of the humans. For now you need to learn of our own kind. And make friends with those who are here."

"But I left without saying goodbye. I want to tell her I'll be moving away. And maybe, with your permission, I could see her from time to time."

She could tell the way his frown lessened he was giving in to her wishes. Inwardly, she smiled. For whatever reason, he seemed to love her despite the fact she was the product of a fae he didn't approve of. Though her father had become a king as well.

"All right, Alicia. You will have three days to spend on South Padre Island with your human friend. But then you must return here."

She hugged him warmly. "I will...oh, thank you. I will."

Her unbridled enthusiasm seemed to please him, and he smiled back. "Three days," he warned, "or the dragon fae will descend on the human world with a vengeance."

"I will return," she promised.

For two hours, she tried to convince someone to take her to South Padre Island, but either the king ordered no one to agree, or they just didn't want to. Her mother couldn't because of the retaining collar she still wore. And even the countess refused her, three times.

Was it because they had lost her to the human world before and if something happened to her, her grandfather would have them killed?

For an hour, she concentrated on trying to transport herself. And then it happened. She nearly fainted. Blackness swirled around her, and she envisioned being home in her bedroom, on her bed. As soon as she arrived, she lay still, trying to orient herself to the spinning room. Once her stomach and gray matter settled, she bolted out of her house and dashed down the street to her friend's.

When she reached Cassie's home, she wiped the memories from Cassie's parent's minds that Viviana had returned Cassie home. Afterward, Alicia transported Cassie to their hotel in South Padre Island.

The hotel staff graciously accommodated them with a new room after Alicia used a minimum of fae mind magic. And Cassie never knew she'd ever left the island.

The day was more glorious than before. The strong sun beat down on the beach as Cassie lay out on her seal beach towel. Alicia jumped up from her lion towel. "Sodas, Cassie?"

"Yeah, sure would be nice."

Alicia slipped a couple of dollars out of a money pouch. She stifled groans as she ran across the hot sand, burning her feet.

As soon as she reached the refreshment stand, she asked for two drinks.

The young man grinned at her. Tall, blond, beautiful tan, and the most gorgeous blue eyes studied her. "Looks like your friend just picked up a date. I'm working until two this afternoon. Want to go out for a burger then?"

Alicia turned to see who Cassie had reeled in this time.

Deveron, wearing only a pair of blue swimming trunks, his tanned skin glistening with water droplets, towered over Cassie. He spoke to her, his cheeks dimpled as he smiled broadly, seemingly oblivious to Alicia even being nearby.

"Some other time," Alicia said quickly to the refreshment stand guy. She dropped the money on the counter. Not even waiting for her change, she grabbed the sodas and stormed across the beach to where Cassie flirted with Deveron.

He grinned at Alicia as he caught her eye. His gaze shifted to the sodas, then back to her eyes again. "Good to see you again, Alicia. But you may have been out in the sun a little too long. Your cheeks are positively rosy."

She pursed her lips, wanting to sock him hard.

He cocked a brow. "You weren't thinking of doing anything with those drinks other than drinking them, were you?" He grinned, the same old devilish dark fae smile.

"You know each other?" Cassie asked, sounding disappointed.

"Yeah," Alicia said. "Maybe too well."

Deveron arched a brow.

Then Alicia caught sight of Micala jogging up the beach. He winked at Alicia.

"My friend and cousin, Micala," Deveron said to Cassie as Micala joined them. "Come swimming with me, Alicia, before you do something you regret and I have to get even." He pulled the drinks out of her hands and passed them to Cassie and Micala.

Alicia couldn't help smiling at him.

"There's my faery princess."

"Just you remember it, dark fae." She grabbed his hand and dashed for the water. "Hot, hot, the sand is burning hot."

He grabbed her up in his arms, and she squealed out in surprise. "I'll protect you from the sand."

"But who will protect you from me?" Alicia asked, grinning at him.

"I will beg for mercy."

"*Right.*"

"Okay, so I won't. You're right. It's not a dark fae quality."

She laughed. "I didn't think your mother would have allowed you to visit the human world again so soon after what happened the last time."

"So what happened the last time?" He ran into the water, but still

148

didn't release her when the Gulf rose to his waist. "I found the perfect mate who released me from a marriage to Lorelei."

"Well?"

"She said just this once."

Alicia stared at him not believing a word he said.

He laughed. "I will never be able to get away with anything with you, will I?"

She shook her head.

"Okay, so she doesn't know."

"Oh, Deveron. If your mother finds you've disobeyed her again—"

"Not to worry." He glanced at the beach where three Denkar fae trackers stood talking to Micala. "Or maybe just a little bit." He kissed her lips. "A year will be a lifetime."

"If you flirt with any more female humans or fae, it will go much more quickly for you."

He chuckled. "Your dragon fae personality draws me to you like a parched fae is drawn to a source of water."

The trackers looked in their direction, but instantly blackness swallowed Alicia and Deveron whole.

He was the worst sort of dark fae, all right, and every bit hers for all eternity—well, in another year.

And truthfully, it wouldn't be soon enough.

ABOUT THE AUTHOR

Award-winning author of urban fantasy and medieval historical romantic suspense, ***Heart of the Wolf*** named in **Publishers Weekly's BEST BOOKS OF THE YEAR, NOR Reader Choice for BEST PARANORMAL ROMANCE.**

Terry Spear also writes true stories for adult and young adult audiences. She's a retired lieutenant colonel in the U.S. Army Reserves and has an MBA from Monmouth University and a Bachelors in Business and Distinguished Military Graduate of West Texas A & M. She also creates award-winning teddy bears, Wilde & Woolly Bears, to include personalized bears designed to commemorate authors' books. When she's not writing or making bears, she's teaching online writing courses in the Heart of Texas.

JUN   2012

Made in the USA
Charleston, SC
19 April 2012